Forehead Kiss
By: Jessica Terry

FOREHEAD KISS

First edition. July 20, 2022.

Copyright © 2022 Jessica Terry.

ISBN: 979-8986432120

Written by Jessica Terry.

I'm over here trying to remember how the characters Nyla and Cam initially came to me and am drawing a blank; I think all the late-nights getting this book ready are catching up to me. lol

In any case, I hope this story makes you smile and laugh and feel good, even a little bit. I love writing romances, especially friends-to-lovers.

Thanks so much to my family, church family, friends, readers, and anyone who has shown me support over this writing journey (which I love, despite how it makes me want to pull my hair out at times). I don't take any support for granted.

Chapter 1

How I met Cam – the love of my life, whether he knew it or not – could either be considered really cute or really embarrassing.

I had just left Starbucks, eyes glued to my phone in one hand, munching on a chocolate chip cookie in the other, and trying to sip from the iced latte tucked between my arm and side boob. (This is a good place to note that I am not terribly coordinated, and I knew this, so I should have been focusing on getting where I was going in one piece instead of trying to multitask. I had already bumped into someone and poked myself in the face with the straw a couple of times from trying to sip without looking. But I guess I was hard-headed. Or stubborn. Or delusional).

Either way, I wasn't looking where I was going. I didn't feel I needed to, since I walked this route practically every day. Occasional glances towards the ground kept me from straight slamming into lamp posts or stepping on the backs of people's feet.

Then all of a sudden, a man appeared, sliding his arm around my shoulders, making me jump so roughly I almost dropped my cookie.

"What the hell-"

"Hey, sweetheart," he smiled at me, tweaking my chin. He leaned down and planted a kiss on my forehead.

"Um, I think you have me confused with someone else," I informed him, trying to twist away but he kept a firm hold on

1

my arm. "So either let me go now or I'll start screaming bloody murder."

"That's what I'm possibly trying to save you from."

"What??"

"Just chill out for a second," he instructed with a smile, his eyes looking ahead. "I promise, I'm not gonna hurt you. Just walk."

For whatever inane reason, I did what he said. We were out in the open in broad daylight with lots of people milling around, so unless he was *really* bold, I couldn't imagine he was going to do anything to me right on the sidewalk. I *did* wish my drink wasn't a cold one, though, just in case I needed to throw it in his...admittedly cute face.

He steered me a couple more blocks to a clothing store, opening the door and ushering me inside with a gentle hand to the back. Once inside, he walked me to a corner, glancing over his shoulder as if to make sure we hadn't been followed. I felt like I was in a spy movie.

"Umm..." I hedged, glancing around as I inched away from him. "What the hell was that? Who are you and why are you acting like you know me?"

"I'm Cam. I was right behind you in line at Starbucks."

"Really? I didn't notice."

"Yeah, I know. You weren't noticing your surroundings, either, because there was a man that was eying you as soon as you walked outside. He was heading right for you."

My eyes widened. "Like...he was gonna..." I lifted my eyebrows pointedly.

"Yeah," Cam confirmed my silent question. "Like he was gonna try to snatch the purse that was hanging halfway down your arm. Or you."

I gasped. "How do you...what...*seriously*??"

"I'm *so* serious. I saw the look in his eye. And you were an easy target since you were buried in your phone; you hardly looked up once while you walked. So I just came over and pretended to be your man to throw him off. As soon as he saw me, he booked it in the other direction."

There was a tiny part of me that still thought I was being pranked, but the shivers overtaking my body were surely real. If what this guy said was the truth, I could've been in some real danger. Realizing how close I'd been to that made me start to freak out a little bit.

"Oh my god..." I panted, my chest starting to heave with panic. The rest of my cookie fell from my hands as I grabbed my chest, clutching the front of my shirt and pacing in a small circle. "*Oh my god!*"

"Hey, hey, calm down," Cam quickly instructed, taking the cup that was still smushed under my arm before I dropped that, too. Setting it on a nearby display, he gently pulled me in for a hug, wrapping some disturbingly comforting arms around me. "You're okay; I've got you."

I buried my face in his chest, letting him comfort me. I felt strangely comfortable with this man I barely knew. He towered over me (as most people did), enveloping me and making me feel safe. His hand rubbed my back in a slow circular motion, and I felt myself melt into him a little bit. It wasn't until I calmed down some that I noticed how great he smelled.

And that he possessed some serious muscles under that shirt and jacket.

Realizing that I was enjoying this a little too much, I made myself step back. My eyes stayed downcast for a few moments, the embarrassment starting to kick in.

"You must think I'm some kind of idiot, huh?" I asked, chewing my bottom lip.

"Nah, not an idiot." He gave me that smile again. He had a dimple in his right cheek. Of course. "But you *should* start keeping your head on the swivel, though. Especially if you're going to be walking around out here by yourself. People are crazy."

"My friend Kori is always telling me that very thing," I admitted, face still shame-burned. "She's forever getting onto me for not looking where I'm going."

"Your friend Kori has a point. And now that I know your friend's name...what's yours?"

"Oh!" I shook my head at myself. Here I was letting this man save my bacon and hug on me and hadn't even bothered introducing myself. "I'm Nyla."

"Hey, Nyla." He took my hand in his, covering it with his other one. "Really nice to meet you."

"You, too. Really. And thank you...*so* much for doing what you did. I'm probably gonna have nightmares about what could've happened if you hadn't."

"Hey, let's just be thankful that all is well."

"I wanna do something to thank you. Can I get you a..." I looked around us, apparently just noticing what kind of store we were in, "...a belt or, like, a gift card...ooh, sunglasses!"

"That's all right," he chuckled, holding up his hands. "You don't have to get me anything. We're good."

"Come on, let me at least try to make this up to you. I know you were just in Starbucks but, seeing as how you don't have any cups in your hands, I'm guessing you didn't get anything. You want a cup of coffee?"

"No thanks. I actually don't drink coffee."

"Oh. Well, tea, then. Or a pastry since I..." Noticing my fallen cookie on the ground. "Need to replace mine."

He chuckled again. "It's really not necessary, Nyla, but if you insist, I'll take you up on the pastry. Starbucks *does* have some bomb brownies."

"Don't they, though?? I almost got one of those, too."

"Yeah, I remember. You kinda went back and forth about it for a minute."

"Wow, you really *were* paying attention, huh?" I muttered, stooping down to pick up my wasted cookie. "And I'll try to do better about that, myself."

"I'm glad to hear it. Now let's go get some brownies."

We headed back outside, and actually ended up spending the next few hours together, opting to go for lunch first before the brownies. By the time we parted ways, we were complete with each other's condensed life stories and contact information.

And I was totally in love.

Cam had no idea because I hadn't had the nerve to tell him. Our friendship had grown and strengthened in the months since we met, and I knew he loved me. But his love was more of the big brother variety, not the kind that involved fantasies of hot oil massages and lengthy makeout sessions like mine was.

My BFF Kori repeatedly (*repeatedly*) pushed me to let Cam know about my feelings but I didn't want to ruin things and humiliate myself, because believe me when I tell you that the day we met wasn't the last time I'd done that in front of him. I *was* still clumsy, after all.

I figured having him in my life as an incredibly sexy male best friend was better than nothing.

"Daydreaming about Cam again, huh?" Kori surmised, leaning over the top of my cubicle at Bryton Communications, aka BryCom, the telecommunications company where we worked. She giggled when I tried to hurriedly start typing on my computer. "Girl, stop, you're caught. Just give it up."

If it were anyone else, I'd have totally denied that I was sitting there thinking about Cam (shirtless in an apron). But I'd whined to Kori enough about my lopsided feelings that there was no point.

"Ready for lunch?" I asked her, checking my watch.

"Yeah. Though you really don't have to do this, girl."

"Hush. This is your last day before you go strike out on your own. That's something to celebrate."

"We're going for tacos, not out on the town."

"Please, you know you prefer tacos."

"True enough," she shrugged. "And I'm good and hungry, so let's roll."

I locked my computer, grabbed my purse, and we headed out. When we had gotten our usual greedy order from our favorite food truck, we sat at one of the nearby tables outside.

"Are you nervous about starting your own business?" I asked her, applying more of my favorite berry-scented lip gloss.

"A little, but also excited," Kori admitted. "I've been wanting to do my own thing for a while now. BryCom was just a means to an end."

"I'm so proud of you. I doubt I'd ever have the nerve or the courage."

"If there was something you wanted to do that badly, you would."

"Maybe I'll start by going for a promotion or something first. I'm sure some positions will be opening up at some point."

"That would be good. *Or* you could go for that man you love. Or both."

I looked at her, sighing. "You know the deal with that, Kori."

"That you're a scaredy-cat?"

"*No*. That Cam doesn't look at me in the *yeah-she's-my-friend-but-she-could-be-my-wife-one-day* sort of way. I'm like the little sister he feels the need to over-protect."

"How do you know? Has he said that?"

"Of course he hasn't said it. But I can tell by how he treats me. There's no flirtations or sexual innuendos or hints about maybe taking things deeper. I've never caught him eying my body or slipping any 'accidental' touches. I'm just a friend to him."

"You're like his *best* friend."

"And I'm thankful for that. So I'll just leave well enough alone."

"I'm telling you, you're going to be sorry when he meets someone and you're left on the sidelines pining, wishing you'd spoken up." She stretched her lengthy legs out in front of her and leaned back, her long braids hanging over the back of her chair. "I'm saying; just because he hasn't made it clear doesn't mean he doesn't feel anything. Men are *great* at hiding their feelings."

Thankfully, our tacos were suddenly ready. I jumped up to get our order, hoping this put an end to this latest round of this particular conversation. Yes, I loved Cam. Yes, I was *in* love with Cam. But that didn't mean anything should be done about it. I considered it an out-of-control crush that was my problem to deal with.

I'd gotten very good at convincing myself of this. And I pretty much believed it.

Chapter 2

"*Why* are you naked??"

My roommate Jada removed one of her earbuds and turned off the vacuum cleaner. "What did you say?"

"I *said* why don't you have any clothes on? Who cleans the house naked??"

"I always clean naked. It makes you concentrate more."

"Huh?? What kind of logic is *that*?"

"Try it. I bet you'll see what I'm talking about."

My head was turned, not needing to see her (admittedly amazing) naked body pushing a vacuum around my living room. "Okay, new house rule..."

"Ugh, *another* one?" she groaned, briefly throwing her head back. "You sure do have a lot of those."

"You make them necessary. Jada, I want you to be comfortable here and everything, but save this kind of boldness for your bedroom. No naked housecleaning."

"What about-"

"That includes cooking."

"Damn." Jada shook her head as she stalked to her room, muttering something about me being a stick in the mud.

Well, sorry that I wasn't free enough to want to scrub toilets in the nude. Or see my roommate do it.

This roommate thing was going to take some getting used to. Jada was a friend of a friend who needed a place to stay, and I needed someone to help with the increased rent. She was a few years younger than me, and it often showed. We had next to nothing in common and probably wouldn't have anything to do with each other in any other situation. And I could tell she was going to require some more acclimation time.

But she could reach BFF status like Kori and I'd *still* be telling her to put some clothes on.

Now, if *Cam* wanted to come dust my shelves wearing nothing but some shea butter, I wouldn't have a problem with it.

Speaking of Cam, he called a little while later, to my complete and utter delight.

"What you doing?"

"Just got home a little while ago. Why, what are *you* doing?"

"Trying to decide what liquor I'm gonna have. And what I'll eat with it."

"Isn't it usually the other way around?" I chuckled.

"Not after the day I had. Come hang with me."

"Sure, yeah, I could go for some booze. Just let me take a shower and I'll meet you at your place."

"*Or* I could come pick you up."

"Not necessary," I quickly protested. "I'd rather just meet you."

"What's up with that?" Cam asked me. "Every time I've offered to swing by there recently, you give me an excuse not to. What's the deal?"

"I just wanna drive my own car, that's all. There's no *deal*."

There was a deal. I never had a problem with Cam coming by before, but then Jada moved in. And where I'm short and busty and adorable, Jada is leggy and luscious and gorgeous. And in the time I'd been friends with Cam, I knew he preferred one over the other, and it wasn't the first one. One look at Jada and I'd be demoted to third wheel status.

"Can you please just let me come get you for once?" Cam persisted. "Plus, I want to see what you've done with the place; you said you got your HGTV-on up in there."

"It's nothing all that spectacular. Just some plants and new curtains and an art wall. I can send you pictures."

"You hiding a refugee in there or something? What's up with the resistance all of a sudden?"

I sighed. He was going to keep bugging me about this until I gave in; I knew it. Maybe Jada would leave before he got there; she always seemed to be out and about.

"Fine," I finally relented. "Just let me know when you're downstairs and I'll-"

"Yeah, nice try. See you in about an hour."

Damn it.

I trudged to my bedroom to see what cute-but-not-trying-too-hard outfit I could put on. I'd just decided on a fitted t-shirt and some hip-hugging dark jeans when Jada appeared in my doorway. Thankfully now clothed.

"You're going out?" she asked, eyeing me as I rifled through my underwear drawer.

"Yep."

"Got a hot date?"

That would be nice. "No...just hanging with my friend, Cam."

"I've heard you mention this Cam guy a few times," she noted, folding her arms. "What's up with him?"

I shrugged a shoulder. "He's a friend. Not much else to tell."

"Is he cute?"

Cute. Fine. Achingly hot. "He's all right."

"Is he coming here? Maybe I'll get to finally meet him."

"Ehh. If he does come up here, it'll only be for a minute. And anyway, I'm sure you have better things to do than meet a friend of mine that you'll immediately forget about. You don't have plans tonight?"

"Not sure yet."

"You should go out, anyway. It's such a nice evening. And now that you're dressed and everything, you might as well head out *now*. Paint the town red, and all that."

"I don't like going out by myself."

"No? You really should consider it. It's very freeing."

"Ugh. I might just stay in tonight and give myself a pedicure. Or maybe I could tag along with y'all."

"Maybe we can do that one day but not tonight," I retorted, trying to sound smooth and not frantic. That was the *last* thing I wanted to happen. "We kind of have our own stuff planned already."

"Bummer," she shrugged, pushing from the doorjamb and flinging her wavy brown hair. "Maybe I'll get to meet this Cam next time."

"Yeah, maybe." *Not.*

After I took a quick shower and quickly ran a flat iron through my short hair, I checked my watch and felt my anxiety rise when I realized Cam would be arriving in the next few minutes. Jada was still home, evidenced by the loud music coming from her room (new house rule alert) and it was my only prayer that she'd fallen asleep. Maybe it was crazy of me, but I just did not want her and Cam to meet, though I knew if she stayed my roommate for any significant time, it would happen eventually.

Soon Cam was knocking on the door. I rushed to it, hoping Jada didn't hear it over her music.

"Hey," I greeted, breathless and grinning. My purse and keys were already in my hand. "Let's go!"

"Hold up," Cam stopped me before I could step out, amused. "You gonna let me in?"

"You need to use the bathroom or something?"

"No, Nyla, I don't need to use the bathroom. I wanted to see your decorating skills, remember? And since when do you listen to rap?"

I don't. "It's really not anything all that major, Cam. I told you; I just put up some curtains and got some new plants-"

"You must be Cam."

Shit!

I forced a smile onto my face as I turned to face Jada, who was standing in the living room eying Cam like a cashmere sweater on clearance. And, when I glanced at Cam, he was equally as enamored. Of course.

Because that's just how much my luck *sucked*.

"Yeah." I sighed as I turned around. "Jada, this is Cam. Cam, Jada."

"Jada." Cam stepped around me, his hand already out. Their eyes were glued to each other. "*Very* nice to meet you."

"Likewise." She eyed him up and down. "Definitely, likewise."

"You a new friend of Nyla's or something?"

"I'm her roommate."

"Roommate?" Cam turned questioning eyes to me. "You didn't tell me you got a roommate."

I shrugged, all enthusiasm for this evening gone. "Never came up, I guess."

"We talk damn near every day, Nyla. How could the fact that you have such a..." He turned back to Jada, his intrigued smirk returning. "...*beautiful* woman living with you not come up?"

"Well, now you know," Jada flirted, leaning closer to him. "So what are you gonna do about it?"

"I'm gonna make sure we stay in touch, that's for sure."

"You know where I live." Jada gently touched a finger to his chest. I resisted the urge to roll my eyes, though it's not like they would have noticed if I had, anyway. I'm sure I was forgotten already. "We'll see what you do about it."

"Oh, don't you worry about that," Cam promised her. "Now I have even more reason to come over here."

"Oh goody," I muttered, cutting my eyes at them.

"Nyla, girl, you didn't tell me your friend was this hot," Jada said to me, eyes still on Cam. "You said he was just 'all right.' It's almost like you wanted to keep him all to yourself."

"Don't know what I was thinking." Over it, I dumped my keys back into the bowl by the door. "You know what? Since you two are so mesmerized by each other, I'm just gonna go to my room and eat some frosting."

"No, no; you two should still go out," Jada insisted, glancing at me. "Don't let me interrupt your plans."

"It's fine. I'm tired, anyway."

"Nyla!" Cam called out when my hand was on my bedroom doorknob. "Come on, we can go. There'll be plenty of time for all of us to get to know each other better." He grinned at Jada. "Right?"

Jada returned his grin. "Absolutely right."

He kissed her hand before finally stepping back, and Jada winked at him before sauntering to her room, no doubt aware that Cam was watching her. Once she was in her bedroom, he looked at me in amazement, mashing a hand to his chest. You'd think dude just won the lottery.

"You have been holding out on me," he happily accused. "I don't know why you've been keeping her under wraps."

"Umph. I had my reasons. Anyway, Cam, I wasn't kidding about being tired, so I'll...call you tomorrow."

"Wait, what's wrong?" He came towards me, concern overtaking his expression. "You were fine a minute ago."

"Yeah, I know. But now I just want to go to bed."

"You aren't upset that I was hitting on your friend, are you?"

Yes. I swallowed. "Why would I be upset? And she's not my friend; she's just my roommate. For the time being. And anyway, it's not like you ignoring me when you see a good-looking woman is anything new."

"Come on, I don't do it *that* much," he dismissed, then eyed me. "Do I?"

"Yeah, Cam, you do."

"Damn. I really am sorry; I don't mean to do you like that. Let me make it up to you. We'll eat, get *wasted-*"

"I *cannot* be doing that; I have work tomorrow," I reminded, pointing a finger at him while trying to hold back a smile. "And you do too, by the way."

"Whatever. Come on; I've been looking forward to hanging with you. I'll get you all the ginger martinis you want."

"Don't be trying to bribe me with ginger martinis." I rolled my eyes and giggled when he hit me with the puppy dog look. "Fine, you nut, let's go."

Cam might have apologized for occasionally hitting on other women while we hung out, but clearly that didn't include *talking* about other women while we were out, because the entire time we were at J.R. Cricket's he was grilling me for information about Jada. Where is she from, how old is she, does she have a man, has she brought any men in there since she moved in with me, what does she sleep in...it was one question after another. I hadn't seen him this hyped about anything since he got promoted to Head Sportswriter. Or the time he won a hundred bucks on a scratch-off.

There weren't enough ginger martinis in existence to make this torture worthwhile.

"Talk me up to her," he urged, grabbing another chicken wing and tearing it apart. "Let her know your boy is worth spending some time with."

"You don't need me for that. I'm sure your natural charm will win her over."

"You're right," he smiled, apparently not recognizing what I thought was clear sarcasm. "We seem to have a connection already. I should've gotten her phone number before I left there. Can you give it to me?"

"Don't start trying to make me your go-between, Cam. I don't want to be involved in y'all's stuff."

"Maybe she'll still be up when I take you home. I'll get it then."

"I'm sure you will."

"Did you tell her how we met?"

"No. Jada is cool but I told you, we're not friends. We don't really talk like that."

"I still don't know why you never told me you had a roommate."

"I mentioned that the rent was going up and I'd likely need to get one, as much as I hated to. How it came to be her happened kind of quickly. She hasn't been there that long."

"Well, I'm damn sure glad she is now," Cam commented. He reached across the table and bumped my fist with his. "Good job on that one."

Yeah. Yay.

"Is there any bad stuff I should know about?" he asked me. "Bad habits, suspicious-sounding phone conversations that might hint that she's hiding something...anything like that?"

I guess this would've been my opportunity to downtalk Jada and make her sound as unappealing to Cam as I could. It wasn't like she and I were close and I owed her anything. I didn't even think I'd feel all that guilty about it.

But that wasn't me. Jada might've been a little nosy and inconsiderate with how loud she was and was a little too uninhibited for my taste, but that didn't make her a bad person.

And I was pretty sure Cam wouldn't find the naked housework thing as unappealing as I did.

"No," I sighed, hating my conscience right then. "Nothing that I know of."

"Good." Cam grinned, looking like he was plotting already. "That's *real* good."

I just downed the last of my martini, somehow knowing things weren't going to be the same from then on out.

Chapter 3

Even through the music, I could hear Cam and Jada getting busy in her bedroom.

It had only been a few days since they met. As soon as I had gotten home that night, Jada was all over me for information about Cam, gushing over him as hard as he'd been about her. She begged me to hook them up after I (reluctantly) assured her there were no baby mamas or secret wives to worry about, and that he was gainfully employed with his own place. After significant hounding, I passed her contact information on to Cam, and he wasted no time using it. Now I was in my living room with pillows over my head trying to act like I couldn't hear them having sex twenty feet away from me.

Why they couldn't go to his place for this was beyond me.

Maybe it was unreasonable of me to expect him to, but Cam didn't even ask how I felt about him getting with my roommate. Even if I *had* repeatedly stated that Jada and I weren't friends and that I didn't care about his initial flirtations with her (that second part a blatant lie, but whatever), it still would've been nice if he had at least asked if I felt some kind of way about it.

Cam was a great friend to me. But he could be a little woman-crazy. Never a cheater, at least not since I'd known him; but rational thought seemed to leave the building when it came to a hot woman. At times, he could actually be kind of an idiot.

My phone lit up beside me, and I quickly grabbed it. I didn't even mind that it was my ex calling.

"Kendrick?"

"Nyla, what's going on over there? Having a party and didn't invite me?"

"You could say *I* wasn't invited, either," I muttered, cutting my eyes at Jada's bedroom door.

"Huh?"

"Nothing. What are you calling me for?"

"I wanna see you. Are you busy tonight?"

"Not at all." I tossed the couch pillows aside and stood, hurrying to my room. "I can be over there in about thirty minutes."

"Damn...I thought I was gonna have to do more convincing than that. Cool; I'll be here."

"All right." I hung up and hurriedly changed out of the shorts and camisole I was wearing into a romper and some sandals. Agreeing to Kendrick so readily probably wasn't the best thing to do because he might've gotten the wrong idea, but these were dire circumstances. He gave me an excuse to get away from the torture of hearing the man I wanted sexing my roommate when it was *my* thighs I wanted him in between.

I didn't let myself think about how meeting up with Kendrick probably wasn't the best idea, period. We usually ended up at odds over something. But I wasn't interested in thinking rationally for the time being; I just wanted to get away from Cam and Jada's sounds of sex and laughter.

Without letting either of them know I was heading out (as if they'd care right then, anyway), I left and headed for Kendrick's. As soon as I got to his place, he pulled me to him and laid a big kiss on me. I allowed it for a few moments before I placed a hand on his chest and stepped back.

"This *isn't* what I came over here for," I informed, eying him pointedly.

"Doesn't mean we can't do it, though." He reached for me again.

"Kendrick, stop." I sidestepped his arms and entered his apartment. "What smells so good? And please don't try to say it's me."

"You always think you know what I'm gonna say," he muttered, closing the door.

"It's because I usually do. You tend to get to know people after being in a relationship with them for two years."

"Uh-huh. Anyway, that's garlic shrimp pasta that you smell."

"Why are you trying to seduce me?"

"I just figured you'd be hungry when you got here, that's all. Wouldn't want to invite you over and not feed you."

"Right." I cut my eyes at him as I put my purse on the couch. "Well, that's nice of you."

"It should be about ready," Kendrick announced, striding towards the kitchen. "Take your shoes off; get comfortable."

Figuring I might as well since I was there, I slid out of my sandals and went to wash my hands. Smelling the aromas coming from Kendrick's kitchen only reminded me that I hadn't eaten in hours. And if I couldn't give Kendrick credit for anything else, I could absolutely give him props for his cooking. He loved to cook. And eat. Which explained his offensive lineman size.

We were about to sit down and eat when my phone started buzzing. My hand automatically started to grab it when I saw it was Cam, but I stopped myself. He hadn't been worried about me when he got to my place and barely spoke before letting Jada pull him into her bedroom. So I wasn't going to pause anything for him now.

"Why are you ignoring your phone?" Kendrick asked, eying it as it started buzzing again. "Ghosting a new man or something?"

"No. It's just Cam; I can talk to him later."

"Oh. Cam," he grunted, sliding my plate over to me. "You never used to ignore his calls around me before. He must've pissed you off."

"Do you care?"

"Not even a little bit. You're on *my* time now."

"Uh-huh. Just eat your food, Kendrick."

As usual, we didn't talk much as we ate. Which gave me opportunity to peek at Cam's texts that were filling up my screen, asking where I was and why I didn't let anyone know where I was going. Guess he and Jada were taking a water break.

"You want some more?" Kendrick asked once I'd cleaned my plate.

"I'm good for now. I appreciate it; it was really good. As usual."

"You know I can put it down in the kitchen." He stood and grabbed my plate, winking at me. "Do I need to remind you how I do in other rooms, too?"

"I've blocked any memories of your bathroom activities."

"Always got jokes. You know what I meant."

"Speaking of the bathroom, I'll be right back," I said, suppressing a smile while I backed my chair from his small table. Grabbing my phone, I headed down the hall for his bathroom, praying it was decent and he'd remembered to flush. It's amazing how much he forgot to do that when we were dating.

As soon as I closed the door behind me, my phone buzzed again with a call from Cam. I just shook my head as I went on about my business, relieving myself and washing my hands before making use of some of Kendrick's mouthwash. When I got a third call in as many minutes, I finally snatched the phone up.

"*What*, Cam?"

"Where are you?" he demanded. "We came out and you were gone!"

"So?"

"*So* you didn't let anybody know you were going anywhere!"

"What am I, fifteen? I don't need to run anything by y'all."

"Where are you, Nyla?"

"Why are you worried about it, Cam? I'm fine."

"Because I don't want anything to happen to you, that's why."

"I'm not out roaming the streets buried in my phone. I've told you, you don't have to baby me because of that one misstep."

"It's not about babying you, Nyla, it's about looking out for you like a friend is supposed to do. And when you're here one minute and gone the next-"

"Which, as a grown woman, I'm more than within my rights to do..."

"Whatever. You could've at least left a note or sent a text or something."

"Cam, you know what? You weren't worried much about me when you were..."

He paused. "When I was what?"

"Nothing," I sighed. "Never mind."

"Hey Nyla!" Kendrick called out from the hallway, banging on the door. "You okay in there?"

I squeezed my eyes shut in frustration. Cam was surely gonna be on my back now because there was no way he didn't hear that.

"Yeah, I'm fine," I let Kendrick know.

"Who the hell is *that*??" Cam exclaimed. "You're out with another dude??"

"Yeah, so?"

"Since when are you dating somebody??"

"Cam, shouldn't you still be banging my roommate and ignoring me like you were before? I'm surprised you even noticed I was gone!"

He got quiet for a moment. "Wait, is *that* was this is about? Nyla, I wasn't trying to ignore you. It's just that-"

"Cam, come back to bed," I heard Jada's voice in the background. "You said to give you five minutes and it's been ten. Now you owe me another round with the handcuffs."

"Oh god," I muttered. I didn't even want to think about whether Jada would be getting cuffed or if Cam would.

"Nyla, when are you coming back? We can talk about this."

"Nothing to talk about. You don't owe me anything, Cam. We're just friends, right?"

Before he could respond, Jada yelled for him again. Cam sighed and I wondered if she was getting on his nerves like she tended to get on mine.

"I'd better go," Cam finally said, his voice low. "You gonna be back soon?"

"I don't know. Probably not."

He sighed again. "Just be careful, okay? Let me know when you get home."

"You mean in case you're not still there? I'll think about it."

There was another long pause before Cam finally clarified, "In *whatever* case. I want to know you're safe, so let me know when you get home. Please?"

I couldn't help but soften a little bit. Cam might have been a pain in my ass sometimes but I knew it was only because he cared about me. Even if he did tend to act like an annoying big brother.

"Fine, Cam. I'll let you know when I'm home safe and sound."

"Thank you." He hung up.

"Nyla!" Kendrick called out again, with more bangs on the bathroom door.

"I'm coming!" Between the two of these men, I should've just gone to a movie or something and turned my phone off.

When I emerged from the bathroom, Kendrick had taken his shirt and jeans off and was posted up on the couch in nothing but his boxers and socks. He patted the spot on the couch next to him.

"Come sit down," he invited, eying me.

I rolled my eyes. "Whatever it is you're trying to do, Kendrick, it's not gonna work."

"I just want you to sit down with me."

"And then what?"

"I'm not plotting anything. Just trying to chill with you."

"Uh-huh." I went and joined him on the couch, but on the far end of it. Kendrick wasn't slick. Nor was he very smooth. It was often easy to tell what he was up to from a mile away.

"Mama asked about you today," he informed me. "Said she wishes she could see you."

"That's nice of her to say. How's she doing?"

"She's all right. Finally on the right diabetes medication. And still on my back about us getting back together."

"And what did you tell her?"

"I told her that was on you. You're the one that broke up with me in the first place; if it was up to me, we'd be planning a wedding by now."

"Right."

"Why don't you call her?"

"Because - as I've told you more than once, Kendrick – your mama is a very nice woman but she's basically just the female version of you. And I don't need *two* people trying to pressure me back into a relationship that clearly didn't work."

"It could've worked, if you tried harder."

"Oh, you think I didn't? I gave you chance after chance, Kendrick, and you know it. I kept telling you about the issues and concerns I was having, and you didn't take it seriously. Then you tried to sic your mother on me. And I got tired of it. So when I ended things with you, I ended things with her."

"I think I should get another chance. Enough time has passed."

Sighing, I ran my hands down my face. I remembered why I broke up with Kendrick and why I'd distanced myself from him for a while afterwards; he always wanted to gloss or skip over the raw facts and just focus on what *he* wanted.

"I didn't come over here to talk about this," I reminded him. "Can't we watch a movie or play some cards or something?"

"If we do watch a movie, can we cuddle?"

"Kendrick."

"What? There's nothing wrong with that. It doesn't have to mean anything, if you don't want it to. I just like you being next to me."

I should've just gotten up and left. But I didn't have money to waste on gas just driving around. I already knew Kori wasn't home. And there was no telling when Cam and Jada would be done with their loud fornicating. Especially since they had another round with the handcuffs to go.

"Fine," I finally relented. I pointed a warning finger at him. "But behave."

"Perfect behavior," he assured with innocently raised hands. As if.

I slid over to where we were touching shoulders, and he immediately put an arm around me. No big deal. He grabbed the remote with his other hand and turned on Netflix before dropping it in my lap.

"You choose."

I glanced at him curiously but his eyes were on the screen, patiently waiting on me to choose something to watch. One of our most played-out arguments when we were together was over Kendrick's staunch unwillingness to share the remote. He always had to be in control of it, like letting go of the remote had some kind of deeper meaning to him. But I surely didn't take him letting me choose a movie one time as any kind of sign.

"This is a good one," I said with a smile, finally settling on something and laying the remote between us. "I've been wanting to check this out for a while."

"A thriller? Figures you'd try *not* to pick something romantic."

"I don't watch a lot of romantic movies; you know that."

"Oh, I know. I remember how you used to tease me when I watched 'em."

"I didn't...never mind. Is this movie okay or do you want me to pick something else?"

"No, this is fine. I'll just close my eyes on the parts I don't want to look at."

"Whatever, Kendrick."

We started watching the movie and it only took a few minutes for me to settle in and get relaxed. I managed to forget about Cam and Jada and just enjoy the moment. After a while, I even let myself forget about my issues with Kendrick and lean closer to him, tucking myself under his arm.

"You good?" he asked, his voice low.

"Yeah."

His large hand gently rubbed my shoulder and I felt myself relax even more. My cheek was pressed against his chest, inhaling his usual Irish Spring scent (seriously, he refused to use any other soap) and resting my hand on his rounded stomach.

I felt him kiss the top of my head and I momentarily closed my eyes, but kept watching the movie.

When a guy came on the screen that resembled Cam, my mouth opened a little in shock. Bald head, adorable puppy dog eyes, teak brown skin, even the dimple; I thought I was dreaming. And the more I watched him kick butt on the screen, searching for the men that kidnapped his sister, I felt myself getting increasingly turned on. It wasn't unlike some of the many fantasies I'd had about Cam since we met.

Which can only explain why I suddenly jumped Kendrick, climbing up his big body like a jungle gym and laying a deep kiss on him. He didn't hesitate to kiss me back, wrapping both arms around me and squeezing. I moaned loudly, my mind imagining that I was making out with Cam, despite the fact that Cam and Kendrick were built totally different. Where Cam was smooth and solid and muscular, Kendrick was big and softer and hairier. My imagination didn't care, though. I rubbed my body against Kendrick's, exhaling when he grabbed handfuls of my ass.

"Lemme get on top," he breathed, trying to push himself up.

I ignored him, pushing my tongue further down his throat. Changing positions might make me come to my senses, and I wasn't quite ready for that yet. I was trying to enjoy this, dammit.

"Nyla..." His hand slid under the hem of my romper.

"Yes," I whispered against his lips, reaching between us to grab his dick. He growled, loving it, as I started stroking the way I knew he liked. It felt so good to get lost in the moment like this.

When he unzipped the back of my romper, my eyes opened. I looked down and saw Kendrick's brown bearded face instead of the one in my head, and immediately started to cool off. I pushed myself up and slid off of him, touching my fingertips to my mouth and adjusting my clothes.

"What's up?" Kendrick asked, sitting up. He put a hand on my thigh. "Why'd you stop?"

"I should go, Kendrick," I muttered, standing. "It's getting kinda late."

"So?"

"So...I don't wanna fall asleep over here. I have to get up early."

"I can wake you up."

"*No*, Kendrick."

"Don't be snapping at me. You're the one that started this, remember? *You* jumped *me*. I was just gonna sit and watch the movie like you said. And now all of a sudden you're acting like *I* did something wrong."

I sighed and looked over at him. He was right. It was on me for letting my imagination run wild just because an actor in the movie we were watching reminded me of Cam.

Clearly, I needed to get it together.

"You're right," I admitted, running a hand over my short black hair before reaching back to zip my clothes back up. "I *did* start it and I shouldn't have. Sorry about that."

"You don't hear me complaining."

"I should still go. We need to leave well enough alone and us having sex isn't doing that."

"Nyla, come on; we're grown. And unless there's something you haven't told me, we're both single. There's nothing wrong with us gettin' down if that's what we both wanna do."

"We might *wanna* do it but we don't *need* to." I went over to get my shoes.

"Who says?"

"Kendrick, just...let it go, all right? It's not gonna happen."

He just eyed me as I put my sandals on and grabbed my purse and keys. I started to head for the door when he called out to me.

"Not sure what's going on with you or what you keep running from, but I hope you figure it out."

I just glanced at him, mildly surprised at the accuracy of his words. I'd come over there in the first place because I was trying to get away from being around Cam doing to someone else what I wanted him to do to me. Then I tried to do to someone else what I wanted to do to *him*. What a mess.

Instead of admitting any of this to Kendrick, though, I just thanked him for dinner and walked out, hoping that the sex show would be over by the time I got home.

Chapter 4

"I still cannot *believe* you hooked them up. Sometimes I think you *try* to shoot yourself in the foot."

I sighed. "For the tenth time, Kori, I did not hook Cam and Jada up."

"You might as well have."

"All I did was be honest when they were each asking me about the other. How is that hooking them up?"

"While you were spewing all this honesty, you should have been honest with Cam about how you feel about him. That was as good an opportunity as any."

"Yeah, tell him that while he's going on and on about another woman. That's *perfect* timing."

"I bet you wouldn't be all moody and horny now if you had."

"Wow, I wish I lived in your world."

"Seriously, Nyla," Kori said. I could hear cars honking in the background and figured she was driving. "You've wanted Cam since you met him and he has no idea. For all you know, he has feelings for you, too. You never know. Especially with the way you two met; right out of one of those TV movies. He could be the love of your life and you're wasting all this time."

"Believe me, if Cam wanted me like that, he'd have let me know by now. He's a lot of things but he is *not* shy."

"Please don't tell me you think you've gotten men figured out. They don't always do things that make sense. Just because he's bold with other women doesn't mean he'd be that way with you. You two *are* friends, after all."

"This is for the best, I think," I avoided, thumping the arm of the chair in the break room at work. "It's probably time for me to get over this silly crush I have on Cam. It's not getting me anywhere. And with the way him and Jada are always all over each other, it's certainly for nothing. I feel like I'm in high school, crushing on the basketball team captain."

"I dated the captain of the basketball team back in the day. Girl, he was so tall and could jump so high...and *big* ol' hands-"

"Before you start reminiscing about stuff I can't relate to, I need to get back to work. My break is almost over."

"Ugh, I don't miss that place at *all*," Kori muttered. "Starting my own business might be a lot and scary and a risk but at least I don't have to time my bathroom breaks."

"It's not that bad."

"And what do you mean stuff you can't relate to? I know you're not trying to act like you didn't date in high school."

"Sure I did. But just regular guys, not the super-popular ones. I was cool with them but they always saw me as a little sister that they felt the need to look out for, not as a hot date. Sometimes being short and baby-faced sucks."

"But at least you'll never look your age."

"Whooptie-do."

"You need to be straight with Cam," Kori advised. It sounded like she had parked her car; the music that had been playing in the background had stopped. "Because you and I both know you're not going to just 'get over it.' I'm telling you, Cam might have deeper feelings for you than you think."

"I'll keep that in mind. What are you out and about doing?"

"Girl, running these errands. I look forward to when I can afford an assistant to do this kind of tedious stuff. But it's all good; one day I'll have a whole staff of folks."

"You absolutely will. I'm so proud of you, Kori, for real; it takes real guts to do what you're doing."

"I appreciate that; it means a lot. 'Cause I do have my little freak-out moments. But I'm way happier now than I was when I was working there at BryCom. And I knew there was never gonna be a perfect time; I just had to jump in and do it."

"And you're doing it. Before too long, folks are gonna be coming from all over to shop at Sleek."

"From your mouth to God's ears. I'm still tripping that I got Chrisette Clarke to agree to let me sell some of her pieces in my little boutique. I've always loved her clothes."

"Chrisette Clarke?"

"Yeah, remember when I showed you the Instagram page of the guy that makes that amazing furniture, and you said you'd give your kidney to have some of his stuff in your apartment?"

"Oh yeah! Dorian Clarke! He's amazing; now *that's* somebody that needs to have his own HGTV show."

"I don't disagree; he's dope. Well, Chrisette is his wife and she put out her own clothing line; said the birth of their second child inspired it. And it is hot stuff; she already had an online boutique but now she's branching out."

"And you worked your charm on her, I see. I'm not surprised."

"Well, now it's just up to me to make sure she doesn't regret it. I need to quit thinking about it or I'll freak out again. Anyway, I'm about to meet with my cousin whose helping me renovate the store; hopefully there won't be any hiccups this time."

"Fingers crossed."

"You're still helping me with the design part, right? I'm *obsessed* with the ideas you've had so far."

"Of course. I'm certainly no professional but you know I love doing that kind of stuff. It's fun for me."

"Professional or not, you damn sure have a knack for it. I have *none*. It's sad, really."

I chuckled. "Silly. I'll talk to you later. Love ya."

"Love ya back."

I sighed and glanced around the break room, feeling a fleeting sense of exhaustion. Seeing how Kori was breaking out to do her own thing made me wonder if I was just settling by staying at BryCom. I'd been working there seven years and had made it to supervisor, but I admittedly never gave much thought to what I wanted to do beyond that. I wasn't sure I had it in me to be an entrepreneur, but I also didn't know if I wanted to stay where I was forever. If I was honest, I didn't know *what* I wanted to do with myself, career-wise. Which was rather sad since I was in my freaking thirties.

Shaking off those thoughts, I got up to throw away my coffee cup and get back to my desk. I had plenty to do to keep my mind off of my lack of career aspirations. And Cam.

If only the rest of the morning didn't take an abrupt nosedive into crap. I got reamed out in a meeting for my team not hitting their metrics for the second month in a row. Then

I had to go and ream out my team for not hitting their metrics for the second month in a row, only to be met with partial indifference.

After that, it was the fun of dealing with customer escalations, creating complex reports, and at least three calls back-to-back. This was the part of my job that I didn't enjoy very much, dealing with headache after headache. I only took the promotion to supervisor because I didn't have any reason not to. Many days I wished I hadn't, because in my previous position I didn't have to deal with all this mess.

I was thrilled when lunchtime rolled around. My relief was slightly deflated when I remembered that Kori was no longer around to be my daily lunchtime buddy, but I decided to make myself feel better by springing for some Mexican food. That's something I usually waited until the evening to enjoy since it sometimes messed with my stomach, but I figured I'd risk it. The spicy chicken enchiladas would be worth it.

So I went and got my food, deciding to eat at the restaurant by myself. I did think about calling to see if Cam had time to come join me, but our hangout time had decreased since he started seeing Jada. I didn't even know if they were an actual couple or if they were just...*having fun* together, but just about every time I'd tried to call him lately, it went to voicemail or we'd talk for a few minutes before Jada snatched his attention. And he was spending plenty of time at my apartment, but of course, he wasn't there to see me.

It stung that Cam was letting Jada take so much of the attention that he usually had for me. He'd dated other women since we met and it didn't interfere with our friendship (aside from my compressed jealousy). I didn't know what was so different about Jada, but I knew it would be a task to be happy for them if they started declaring love for each other. I didn't want to hear that. It was hard enough when Cam went out with anyone else but it was a double kick to the gut that he was so especially enamored with a woman he likely wouldn't have even met if it weren't for me.

Figuring it couldn't hurt to try, I called him. It eventually went to voicemail, but I didn't bother leaving a message. I already knew he took forever checking them and anyway, he'd see my missed call. Maybe I could make a game out of how long it would take him to call back.

After devouring my enchiladas, refried beans, and rice (and a few too many chips and salsa before that), I headed back to the office, wishing I could just go home. A belly full of delicious food made me want to recline on the couch, not sit at a desk fielding issues from my twelve-person team.

My phone buzzed with another text from Kendrick. He'd been contacting me more than usual since I stupidly climbed him like a rock wall at his place the other night.

I wanna see you. Can you come by later?

Sighing, I put my phone back down, not in a hurry to respond. Kendrick was the type to take a mile when given an inch, so it didn't surprise me that he took what happened at his place to mean more than it did. My little lapse in judgment had opened floodgates that I had spent painstaking months forcibly closing, and I didn't know if I had the energy to go through all that with him again. Kendrick wasn't a bad guy at all; we just weren't a good fit.

"Nyla, are you going to be able to jump on this conference call in a few minutes?" one of my team members, Kristen, poked her head around my cubicle wall and asked. "It's about those account transitions."

"Oh...yeah." I'd totally forgotten about that. "I'll jump on if I can. If not, just give me the rundown later."

"What if they have a lot of questions?"

"Then...answer them."

"I doubt I'll *know* all the answers. And you know the sales reps will be grilling me about every little thing."

I tried not to sigh out loud. My team provided account support for the cellular and data services of business customers, and we worked alongside several other departments, including Sales. And Sales could be a pain in the butt to deal with at times, so I knew if I wasn't on the call to keep them in check, they'd hound Kristen until she screamed (which she had actually done before; right in the middle of the office. It kinda freaked everyone out).

"All right, I'll be on there," I assured her.

Looking relieved, she flashed me a smile and disappeared. I tried not to notice that I hadn't even been back from lunch a full half hour yet.

Another text from Kendrick came in:

We need to finish what we started the other night. Come through.

All I had to do was tell Kendrick that the only reason I started something with him the other night was because I got turned on by Cam's doppelganger on the movie we were watching, and he'd chill out. Would probably be insulted. I was *trying* not to go there.

I'll fix some pork chops.

Wow, he's *really* trying to get me over to his place. Pulling out the big guns with the pork chops.

Figuring I'd better go ahead and answer him, I started typing a response when I felt my stomach start to rumble, and it certainly wasn't from hunger.

"Oh hell..."

Pressing a hand to my belly, I tried to take a few deep breaths, hoping that would make a difference but knowing from experience that it wouldn't. A calendar reminder popped onto my computer screen about Kristen's conference call, and I could only hope that it didn't take that long.

"Good afternoon, everyone," I greeted once I joined the call. "Hope everyone's having a good afternoon so far; let's go ahead and jump in so we can all get on with our day, huh?"

"Thanks for joining, Nyla," Carla, one of the sales managers, greeted me. "I'm glad you're on because we have quite a few concerns to go over."

Great.

I sat there suffering through the entire call, that of course seemed to drag on and on. Every time I tried to steer things towards a conclusion and wrap it up, someone piped up with another question. Or worse, some random comment that had absolutely nothing to do with the topic at hand.

"Hey, I know this is totally random, but has anyone seen that viral video of the deer that ran through that picnic site?" Andrew, another sales rep, asked after I tried to conclude the call for the third time. "That was so funny, how everyone freaked out!"

I'm about to freak out right now, I thought as I shifted in my seat, willing my body to calm down. I *really* needed to get to a bathroom. *And it won't be funny, either.*

"Guys, I'm gonna have to hop off," I finally said, not able to take anymore. "If there's anything else I need to know, just, *ooh*," I winced as a hard rumble tore through my stomach. "Just shoot me an email."

"Okay, will do. Thanks, Ny-"

I hung up and ripped the headset off, standing and turning to head for the door, trying to look like I wasn't about to burst. I was halfway there when I realized I hadn't locked my computer, so I ambled back and hurriedly did that before doing a swift walk for the door, praying nobody tried to stop me to talk.

Thankfully I made it to the elevators unbothered, but knowing what I needed to do, I pressed the button for the elevator to go to the top floor of the building. It might have been silly but I didn't want to risk anyone coming into the bathroom while I was doing my damage, or coming in as I was leaving *after* doing it. I was well aware of how people talked in that office and didn't need to be the topic of conversation for *that*.

As I was waiting in agony, a couple of other people came and joined me by the elevators, engaged in lively conversation about an unfortunate pharmacy experience. I resisted the urge to groan out loud (and hoped my stomach didn't, either).

When the elevator dinged and opened, they both stepped on and looked at me.

"You coming, Nyla?"

"Oh, um...y'all go ahead. I just remembered something I need to grab from my desk."

"Okay," they shrugged, returning to their conversation as the elevator doors slid closed.

"Dammit!" I cursed, ambling towards the door to the stairs. There was no way I could have justified going to the top floor that everyone knew was unoccupied, and I didn't have time to ride down with them and then double-back. I'd just have to clinch-walk it up three flights of stairs and pray for a little more time from the bowel gods.

Managing to make it upstairs without soiling myself, I hurried into the bathroom and started to make a beeline for the stall when I realized I wasn't alone in there.

And I heard the heavy panting before I heard any words.

"Don't stop, I'm close..."

"You said this was gonna be a quickie; can you hurry it up?"

"Are you seriously rushing me right now??"

"Somebody can come in here! Oooh, yes, right there..."

"You like that, huh? And you know nobody ever comes up he-"

"Knock knock."

"Aaugh!"

The screams would have been funny if I wasn't worried about pooping my pants like a toddler.

There were sounds of a lot of fumbling and hushed whispers and things being zipped. The stall doors went all the way to the floor so I wasn't able to see any shoes. I just stood and waited for them to come out, too curious to do anything else. Thankfully my digestive system apparently hit the pause button so I could enjoy this.

"Oh my god...Nyla, hey!" Leslie, who I used to work with before getting promoted, exclaimed when she peeked out of the stall. She hurriedly tried to brush her chin-length hair into place and plaster on a casual smile, despite still being breathless and a tad sweaty. Her papersack brown face was flushed. "What...what are you doing up here?"

"I guess I don't need to ask *you* that, huh?"

"Heh..."

"I'm sure your partner is ready to get up out of that stall so you might as well let him out."

With a deep sigh, Leslie fully stepped out and her stall lover, a guy I recognized but couldn't place, emerged looking sheepish.

"Ma'am," he greeted me, nodding his head.

"Nyla, you know Leo?" Leslie asked me. "He works down in the café."

My jaw dropped slightly. This was the guy that served my tater tots.

"We've never been formally introduced," I muttered, eying him as he tried to subtly tuck his work shirt back into his pants. "At least now I have a name to put with the face."

"Ooh, Nyla, are you meeting somebody up here, too?" Leslie asked conspiratorially, giving me a sly smile. "Can you give us like five minutes-"

"That's *not* why I'm up here," I corrected, holding up a hand. "I, um..." My stomach was starting to remind me in fact why I *was* up there. "I was asked to come and check to see if anybody was..." I wiggled my eyebrows and looked at them pointedly. "You know. Apparently they suspect this might be a hookup spot."

"Are you serious??" Leslie gasped. "You're not gonna rat me out, are you?"

"I told you we should've gone to my car for this," Leo hissed at her with a little nudge. "Nobody would've seen nothin' behind my tinted windows."

"Look, I'm not gonna say anything," I assured them, trying to keep a straight face. "But you might wanna...go on back downstairs, you know. Just in case someone else decides to come check behind me..."

"Okay, yeah...um, let's go, Leo." Leslie scurried out, apparently suddenly bashful since she kept her eyes on the floor.

Leo, in less of a hurry, strolled past me towards the door, giving me another nod. "Ma'am."

I just nodded at him and prayed for them to hurry up.

When I heard the ding of the elevator and poked my head out to confirm they were both gone, I sprinted back towards the stall, slapped a ton of toilet paper on the seat, and *finally* let it all out.

After that nonsense, I decided to just go home for the day. I had more work to do but I decided it could wait.

(But as far as my team and superiors were concerned, I'd be working on some stuff when I got home. Right.)

Thankfully, I got home to an empty apartment. Jada was a department store clerk and sometimes worked weird hours, but I had a feeling that her absence was Cam-related. Not that she and I discussed their relationship; we didn't. But I heard some of her conversations when she was gabbing with her friends; she wasn't exactly discreet. I heard her refer to Cam as her 'boo' several times and it always made me cringe.

Sighing, I changed out of my work clothes, grabbed some juice from the refrigerator and plopped onto the couch. I had just turned on HGTV when my phone rang. I was mildly surprised to see it was Cam.

"Hello? Who is this?" I answered.

"Huh? Nyla, it's me, Cam."

"Cam? Cam who?"

"Why you playing?"

"It can't be the Cam that's supposed to be my boy because I've barely heard from *him* in days. He has this new woman, you see..."

"Okay, okay," Cam conceded. "I figured you'd get onto me about that. I'm sorry for being scarce recently. I know you've called a few times..."

"Yes, I did."

"...And I missed the calls..."

"Nor did you call me back."

"I'm sorry for that," he insisted, sounding frustratingly sincere. "I know I'd feel some kinda way if you did the same thing to me."

"Yes, you would."

"Let me make it up to you. What time are you leaving work?"

"I'm home already."

"Why?" Cam's voice took a concerned tone. "You all right?"

"I'm fine. I'd just had enough of the office for today."

"Perfect. I'm covering the men's basketball game tonight over at State. Come with me."

"Cam, you know I only have marginal interest in sports."

"You'll be hanging with your boy, though, so that means an automatic good time."

"I appreciate the offer, but I just wanna chill tonight. It's been kind of a rough day and I don't feel like being around a bunch of people."

"You're just gonna lay around there watching HGTV and we both know it. Come on, we haven't hung out in a while."

"That's not *my* fault."

"I know, I know..."

"You know what, Cam? You've been different ever since you started messing around with Jada," I blurted out. I wasn't planning on going there but what the hell. "I never used to have to beg for your attention before, even when you were seeing someone else. I get that your boo-of-the-moment gets top billing and all, but this time it's like you've totally just tossed me aside."

He got quiet for a moment. "I-I guess I didn't realize I was that bad about it."

"Yes, you are. And I'm not gonna lie, it hurts. You can't even see how much I..."

My voice trailed off as my momentary hutzpah faded. It wasn't the best time to admit that my feelings for him were not as platonic as he thought.

"What were you about to say?" Cam pressed. "I can't see how much you what?"

"Nothing," I quickly muttered, hating that I'd lost my nerve like that. "It's not important."

"Wait a minute...I think I know what this is about. I know what you were gonna say."

"You do?" I sat up, unfolding my legs and letting one foot drop to the carpeted floor. "Umm, I doubt that."

"Oh no, I'm sure I do. Really, I don't know how I didn't realize it before."

I felt a cold shot up my spine. There was no way he just up and noticed my feelings for him all of a sudden. It wasn't like I was overly flirty with him or left any evidence he could find, like doodles of his name or drawings of what I imagined certain parts of his anatomy looked like.

But...maybe he suddenly realized deeper feelings for *me*? Maybe he had started looking at me differently and it just hit him that I could be more than just the cute short friend that he felt the need to watch out for.

"Realize what?" I asked him, my voice practically in a whisper. My finger nervously twisted around my shirt. "What is it you realize, Cam?"

"That I should just take Jada to my place from now on when we wanna hook up. I figure seeing us together is probably tough for you since you haven't been on a date in a while."

My jaw dropped momentarily before I sucked my teeth.

"Cam," I sighed, turning up the volume on the television. "You're such an idiot sometimes."

"What?"

I just hung up and snuggled in to watch *House Hunters*.

Chapter 5

"We need to talk, Nyla."

It was Saturday morning and too early for this, whatever it was about. I rubbed the sleep out of my eyes and squinted at Jada.

"About what?"

"Can you come out to the living room? I don't want to have this conversation standing here in your doorway."

"Jada, can this wait? It's not even eight o'clock in the morning. Whatever it is can't be that serious."

"Oh, it is. And I'm sorry for waking you up but I have to go to work in a little bit and don't want to wait until I get off. It'll just bug me all day."

"Ugh." I scratched my head through my scarf as I opened my bedroom door wider. "Fine, but can we make it quick?"

"Yeah. I told you, I've gotta go to work, anyway."

"This is a new house rule alert, by the way. If you're gonna wake me up this early on a Saturday, either something better be on fire or LL Cool J better be at the door shirtless and carrying tacos."

"Ugh. *Fine.*"

I followed her to the living room, with her glancing back at me a couple of times to make sure I didn't retreat back to my room and lock the door, I guess. She took a seat on the couch and waited for me to do the same.

"I need to know...what exactly is going on with you and Cam?"

That woke me up. I blinked a few times, shooting her a curious look. "What do you mean? We're friends."

She looked at me expectantly. "And?"

"There's no *and*. That's it."

"Are you sure?"

"How could I *not* be sure, Jada? Is this what you woke me up for?"

"Yeah, because I have to wonder if there's more between you two than you're telling me."

"I don't know why. Because there isn't." *Not because I don't want it to be, though.* "Why are you asking?"

"Because he's been talking about you a *lot* lately," Jada informed me with a slight frown. "Every time we're together, he finds some reason to bring your name up. Asking me what you're doing, if you're seeing somebody now, if you've brought anybody by here. It's always something. We've even argued about it."

Right or wrong, I wanted to grin at that. But I didn't.

"That's too bad."

"And I've seen some of the looks you give us when we're here. Like seeing us together bothers you."

It does.

"I don't know what to tell you, Jada," I replied, keeping a straight face despite my inner twirlings. "There's never been anything between Cam and I but friendship. We haven't even talked much in the last week or so-"

"Why? Y'all have a fight or something?"

"No. Not really. I called him an idiot about something and kinda hung up on him, and we haven't really talked since."

"And it wasn't because he made a move on you? Or you made a move on him?"

"No. No moves have been made in either direction."

"So y'all have never kissed or *anything*?"

"No, Jada. We haven't done anything but hug. The only kisses have been on the forehead. Trust me, there is *nothing* romantic about my relationship with Cam."

"Hmm." She eyed me, as if she was trying to determine if I was full of it or not. "There has to be some reason why he's so interested in what you're doing all of a sudden."

"Who knows. He never likes it when I'm upset with him."

"I just know that it's not a good feeling when my man spends so much time worrying about another woman, regardless of who it is. He should be focused on *me*."

"Tell *him* that."

"Oh, you think I didn't? We argued about it, I told you."

"Sorry to hear that." I paused, part of her earlier comment blaring in my mind. "You called Cam your man, so...y'all are official now? Like, *together*-together?"

"Of course." Her eyes narrowed slightly. "You have a problem with that?"

I shrugged, ignoring the immediate flaming that came over my face at her confirming that. "Why should I care?"

"I just have a feeling you don't approve."

"Even if I didn't..."

"But do you approve or not?"

I sighed, sensing she wasn't going to let this go until I gave her a straight answer. "Fine, Jada, fine. If you *really* want to know...no, I'm not thrilled about it."

She actually looked surprised. "Really?"

"Yeah, really. I don't think you two are a good fit. It's probably nothing more than just sex between you two and I imagine it won't be too long before one of you realizes that and your little fling crashes and burns."

A few tense moments passed. Jada just sat there peering at me, and I wondered why I let myself say all that. Not that I didn't mean it, but I had betrayed my self-made promise of outward indifference towards Cam and Jada's...relationship. But that was out the window now.

I thought Jada was going to explode on me, but a small giggle actually escaped. Then a full-on laugh. Her hand flew up to cover her mouth as she fell against the back of the couch, shaking with laughter.

"Nyla, girl," she finally said between chuckles, "You are too funny. Crash and burn. That's hilarious!"

I wasn't smiling even a little bit but it apparently didn't matter. Jada continued laughing as she stood from the couch.

"I've gotta go to work," she announced, still amused. "I'll see you later."

She left, and I just shook my head, wondering why I didn't just sell an organ instead of getting a roommate.

"This is coming together great, Kori. I can't believe it's almost time for your grand opening."

"Girl, I know!" Kori marveled, her hands on her cheeks as she looked around her near-empty space. The walls had been recently painted a pearlescent metallic gray and new vinyl plank flooring was put in, and they were replacing some light fixtures while we roamed around. "Just a couple more weeks. It's all getting *real*. I'm excited, though."

"I'm excited *for* you. You're really doing it."

"Are you going to be able to make it to the grand opening?"

"Come on, what kind of question is that? Of course I'm gonna be here."

"You bringing Cam?"

"Ugh. I don't know." I folded my arms and hunched my shoulders. "He might be busy, for all I know."

"What do you mean, for all you know? Y'all haven't talked?"

"Not recently."

"What happened?"

"Nothing I feel like getting into. Just Cam being Cam."

"So...clueless when it comes to your real feelings for him, huh?"

"Not just that. I know he's not a mind reader; I can't expect him to just *know*. When it comes to women in general, though, he can be surprisingly dense. And not very perceptive."

"Honey, that's a lot of men."

"Yeah, well. Regardless, I'm not sure if I want to bring Cam. Inviting him might mean indirectly inviting Jada, too. She's already suspicious about the nature of my and Cam's friendship."

"Ooh, why?" Kori whipped her head towards me, long braids flying. "Did she catch you two doing something?"

"Girl, please, we haven't come close to doing anything. It's still just all bear hugs and forehead kisses. I'm telling you, he still sees me like a little sister. I don't see that changing, especially as long as walking sexpot Jada is in the picture."

"Well, then you need to change how he sees you. Take a break from the casual – but admittedly cute – stuff you always wear and spice it up a bit. Wear something that accentuates those boobs. Rock some heels every once in a while. Put on some eyeliner; a good black will make those pretty light brown eyes of yours pop."

"Hmm. Anything else?"

"You know Cam better than I do. What is he attracted to?"

"He's kind of a leg man. So that's a strike against me right there."

"Who says? You might be short but that doesn't mean you don't have nice legs. Let him see 'em more often. And make sure you oil them up real good. Girl, some little cutoff shorts and some platform heels would probably have him salivating."

"I don't think there's enough oil in the state for that."

"You'd be surprised. But if you want something even *more* foolproof, get him good and drunk and then make your move."

I looked at her like she was crazy. And she was. "I can't do that, Kori!"

"What? I'm not saying to get him sloshed and then hump him. Just lay a good kiss on him. One he can't forget, no matter how much cognac is in his system. I bet he won't see you as *lil' sis* anymore."

"And you think one kiss while he's hammered is supposed to change something? He won't even remember it."

"You mean to tell me you don't remember *anything* you've ever done while you were drunk? I'm not talking sloppy, falling-all-over-himself wasted. Just tipsy enough where he won't stop you when you go in but will still remember it once his head is clear."

"You're crazy, Kori. You *do* know that, right?"

"Hey, *I'm* not the one who is miserably lusting after my best man friend and doing nothing about it," she reminded, looking at me pointedly. "You two could be all lovey-dovey by now if you had spoken up sooner, for all you know. *That's* crazy."

I brushed her off, but that didn't mean I didn't inwardly agree with her, at least in part. Truth was, I *didn't* know how Cam would have reacted if I told him about my crush. Just because I hadn't seen him with anyone similar to myself or because he didn't do any sly flirting didn't mean he couldn't find me attractive. Maybe if I put myself out there and let it be known that I saw him as more than a friend, he might start looking at me the same way.

Kori's suggestion about trying something with Cam when he was tipsy ran through my mind again. Even though I'd shot it down when she said it, it wasn't *that* ridiculous of an idea. Cam and I had certainly spent plenty of evenings drinking together. What harm would it do if I kept the drinks flowing more than usual and then planted one on him? I could always blame the alcohol if he wasn't feeling it.

But...then I'd always *remember* he wasn't feeling it.

This foolishness was still on my mind when I got back home. I was running down the mental pros and cons list of coming clean with Cam when I walked into my apartment and screamed my head off, swinging my purse like a weapon as I plunked into the wall.

"Damn, calm down!" Cam exclaimed, shooting off the couch, arms outstretched towards me. "It's just me!"

I pressed a hand to my heaving chest and glared at him. "What the hell are you doing in here??"

"Jada let me in. Though she had an attitude about it, for whatever reason."

I rubbed the shoulder that had hit the wall. "Is she here?"

"No, she had to go in to work."

"So you had her let you in here so you could ambush me? And for the record, this might be why she had an attitude, Cam. What woman enjoys their man asking them to let them into their place so they can be alone with someone else?"

"Jada knows you and I are just friends," Cam dismissed, waving off my suggestion. "And you really didn't leave me any choice, with how you've been ghosting me recently."

I sighed, removing my jacket and dumping it and my purse on the couch. "I haven't been ghosting you, Cam. I've just been busy."

"Too busy for me? I thought I was your boy, Nyla."

I hesitated. "You are."

"So what's up with the cold shoulder all of a sudden? First you hang up on me, then you ignore my calls..."

"I know..."

"When I did that to you, you copped an attitude. What is this, payback?"

Briefly rubbing my temples, I went over to mindlessly check the mail Jada had brought in. "No, it's nothing like that. There's nothing going on."

"Yes, there is. I know you, Nyla." He came over to stand behind me. "Talk to me."

My eyes slid closed at the scent of his cologne. I could actually feel the heat from his body, and it was making me tingle in a way I knew I'd be remembering later in bed.

His hands landed on my shoulders and gently turned me around to face him before he tipped my face up with his finger under my chin. I didn't want to look up into his sexy sleepy eyes but I couldn't *not* look, either.

"If something's wrong, please tell me," he requested, searching my face. "You know I don't like when you shut me out."

I swallowed, trying to compose myself. My hands ached to reach out and slide up and down his stomach to feel the firmness that I knew was there. I hated not being able to touch him like I wanted to and my resentment of Jada for having that kind of freedom with him doubled.

"I'm sorry for having an attitude and not really telling you why," I finally said, briefly averting my eyes before looking back up at him. "That...wasn't fair. I was just upset."

"Upset about what? What did I do?"

You're banging my roommate when I really want you to be hugged up with me. I'm upset because you can't tell I'm in love with you and I'm not sure what you'd do about it if you could.

"I...Cam, it's...it's hard to explain," I stammered, hating that I couldn't just blurt it out. "Just know I'm...I'm dealing with it. It's *my* problem, not yours."

"But if I can help you with it, I want to."

"I don't know if you can. Or if you'd even want to, really."

"Why wouldn't I? What's going on, Nyla?"

"It's nothing, Cam, seriously," I insisted, stepping around him with my eyes squeezed shut. That would've been a good time to come clean but I couldn't bring myself to do it. I wasn't sure if it was because I was more scared of his possible polite rejection or what such an admission would do to our friendship.

"Nyla-"

"Can we please, *please* drop it? At some point I'm sure I'll be ready to talk to you about everything but for now...I'm not ready yet. Can you respect that?"

He turned to look at me, a frown of concern marring his face. "Fine, but at least tell me this much; you're not in any kind of trouble or danger, are you?"

"No. I promise, it's nothing like that."

"All right, then." I could tell he was frustrated that I was being so tight-lipped, but I couldn't imagine he'd been in the situation I was in, wanting someone and too terrified to let them know. Cam was way more self-assured than I was; if the roles were reversed and he confessed feelings to me that I didn't reciprocate, he'd probably either make some kind of joke out of it or write it off as my loss.

"But thank you. For being so concerned and coming to check on me," I told him, giving a small smile. "I really do appreciate that."

"Come on, you know I'm gonna always check on you," he assured me with a wink. "You're my girl. I love you."

My smile turned into a pained one, knowing he didn't mean that the way I wished he did. "I know you do."

"So since I'm here, how 'bout we do something?" He clapped his hands before rubbing them together. "Have you eaten yet?"

"A while ago. I'm not all that hungry right now."

"How about a movie, then? Something scary where you get to bury your head in my shoulder the whole time?"

I couldn't help chuckling. "As much fun as that is, I'm not really trying to get freaked out tonight. We can go watch something else, though, after I change clothes."

"Cool. I'll check showtimes and all of that stuff while you go get ready. Don't be all day, though."

"Hush."

He pulled out his phone and parked it on the couch while I went to my room. While I was rummaging through my dresser, I thought about Kori's suggestion to spice up my outfits around Cam. But he'd surely know something was up if I strutted out there in something too different than what I usually wore, especially just to go to the movies. And I didn't even own any booty shorts.

Opting for my usual cute-sexyish-casual look, I quickly touched up my short hair and refreshed my perfume. I did take one of Kori's suggestions and put on some mascara and eyeliner, along with my shiny berry gloss on my lips. I usually didn't bother with makeup when Cam and I hung out and was curious as to whether he'd even notice it or not.

Cam was still scrolling on his phone when I reentered the living room.

"You ready?" he asked without looking up. "There are a couple of things starting in about half an hour."

"Okay." I stood there, waiting for him to look up. "Is it my turn to choose or yours?"

"Yours. Just don't have me watching any chick flicks."

"When is the last time I did that?" I was still waiting on him to look at me. "What's playing?"

"Come here and see."

Going to sit next to him, close but not touching, he handed me his phone, only giving me a quick glance. "Of the next three showings, there's action, some kind of documentary, and a crime drama. If you choose that documentary, I'll be mad at you for a week."

Laughing, I nudged his leg with mine. "Whatever. I oughta choose it just 'cause you said that. But I'll have mercy on you. Let's go with the action one."

"Good girl," he winked at me, standing. I followed suit, handing his phone back to him. "Ready?"

"Yeah." He still hadn't really taken note of my face; he just checked his pockets for his keys. Sighing, I grabbed my purse. "Let's go."

Cam drove us to the theater and we went straight to the concession stand after getting our tickets, getting in separate lines to get our snacks, per our usual routine. I got the candy, he got the slushies. I tried to peer around the people in front of me to see if there were any peanut M&Ms in the case, because the last time they were out, Cam pitched a whole fit.

A man got in line behind me, but I barely glanced at him. I just hummed to myself and mindlessly twisted side to side while I waited my turn.

"Excuse me; do you have the time?"

It took me a second to realize he was talking to me. I glanced back at him in surprise before checking my watch. "Twelve after eight."

"Cool, thanks."

"Mmm-hmm."

I started to turn back around when he spoke up again. "Is it obvious that I just asked you that to get your attention?"

"What?"

"I could've just looked at my phone," he clarified, pulling it out of his jacket pocket. He was smiling at me. "I'm just not very good at ice-breakers."

Turning slightly, I looked up at him again, this time with attention. He was rather cute, with his curly tapered 'fro, trimmed beard, and nice teeth. And as weird as this was to say about anyone, he had a cute nose.

"Well, I'm not usually that great at them, either," I replied, returning his smile. "But asking for the time is a classic."

"Can't do too bad with the classics. Um, what's your name? I'm P.J."

I saw Cam frowning at us from where he stood in the next line over, and I just shook my head at him. He always started tripping when men stepped to me while we were out. "Nyla. Nice to meet you."

"Same. I like the name Nyla; it's pretty."

"I appreciate that, thank you. It was originally going to be Darla so I'm very thankful for the final decision."

"You'd still be just as attractive, believe me. And I'm sure you hear this a lot, but your eyes are gorgeous."

I smiled, blushing. It had been a little while since someone flirted with me like this and it felt nice. Especially since I found him attractive, too.

We moved up a little in line as we continued to make small talk, with Cam glaring over at us the whole time. I just pretended not to notice.

"You from around here?" P.J asked, stepping a little closer. He was only a few inches taller than me, which meant he wasn't considered tall by normal standards; I was only 5'2, myself. But it was rather endearing to not have to strain my neck looking up at someone for a change.

"Practically. Moved to the area when I was five or six. What about you?"

"I've been here a few years. Moved down here for work. I'm in I.T."

"So you're the man of initials, huh?"

He laughed, rearing his head back. "I never thought of it like that but I guess so. And I'm about to load up on M&Ms in a minute."

Hearing Cam's favorite candy made me remember that he was probably still eyeing us, but I refused to look over at him. If he could sex my roommate while I was in the other room (and after only knowing her a few damn days), I could surely do some mild flirting with a man in a concessions line.

"I'm a gummy worm fan, myself," I informed P.J., taking another step forward in the line. "Extra points for the sour ones."

"Maybe I can get to earn those points if we grab a movie together sometime."

I grinned, blushing harder. "Maybe, yeah."

"I guess I should've asked this already but...are you here with anybody?"

"Yes, you should've," Cam barked, appearing at my side and mean-mugging P.J. He must have gotten out of line just to come over there because he wasn't holding any slushies. "Because she *is*."

"Oh, my bad," P.J. quickly replied, holding his hands up. "I didn't know..."

"No, P.J., you don't have anything to apologize for," I assured, shooting Cam a death glare before turning my eyes back to him. "He and I are *not* on a date; we're *just* friends, believe me."

"Still. Date or not, you came here with *me*," Cam insisted before P.J. could respond. He stepped in front of me, looking at my suitor as if he was daring him to oppose. "And she's gonna leave with me, too, so you might as well go try to run your game on somebody else."

"Cam!"

"Umm, look, Nyla, it was nice to meet you, but I don't want or need any drama. You enjoy your movie." With that, P.J. stepped out of line and headed towards the theaters, apparently no longer having a taste for his M&Ms.

I slowly turned to Cam, breathing fire. He was still watching P.J. as if to make sure he didn't change his mind and come back, then had the nerve to try to grab my hand.

"Come on, let's go ahead and get our seats," he ordered, tugging on me. "I don't even want snacks anymore. I just hope we're seeing the same thing as that busta so he can learn again how he needs to watch who he's trying to mack to."

Wrenching from his grasp, I gave him a hard shove to the chest and stormed off in the other direction towards the exit. Cam was right on my heels, trying to stop me.

"Nyla, hold up!" He managed to take hold of my arm again, stepping in front of me. Again, I yanked away from him. "Where are you going? What's wrong with you?"

"What's wrong with *me*? What the hell is wrong with *you*, Cam, acting like you have some say in who I talk to!"

"Are you seriously mad because I ran that guy off? You didn't even know him!"

"And I guess I never will now, will I? Since you had to come over there acting stupid! Cam, you had no *business* doing that! I am a grown woman, dammit!"

"I know how old you are, Nyla, but that doesn't mean I'm not gonna look out for you. And when I see some *punk-*"

"Did you know that guy, Cam?"

He blinked. "What?"

"Do you know him? The guy that you acted like an asshole towards, do you know him personally?"

"Hell no. How would I?"

"Just like I thought. So you have no way of knowing if he's a punk or a busta or anything else."

He sighed, calming down slightly. "Okay, fine. I'll give you that. But Nyla-"

"Save it, Cam. I am so *pissed* at you right now I seriously want to kick you right in the balls. So just shut up talking to me."

"Are you serious??" He gaped at me, sincerely incredulous. "How am I in the wrong for having your back?"

"I don't need you to be my protector, Cam!" I practically screamed. Several people were looking at us, but I didn't care. "We go out and you see a pretty woman and hit on her in my face and *that's* no big deal, right? But a man *politely* approaches me and you act like you have some kind of claim. Did I act like this when you came over to see me and then *ignored* me as soon as my roommate walked in? No, I did not! You're *with* you wanna be with, Cam; you don't get to dictate who I'm with, too!"

"I'm sorry, okay?" He glanced around at our small audience before turning pleading eyes back to me. My anger didn't budge. "Can we just go see the movie and talk about this later?"

"No, Cam. I don't want to see anything with you. Take me home."

"Nyla!"

"Either take me home or I'll get there myself. Matter of fact, I think I'd prefer that." I pulled out my phone.

"What are you doing?" He tried to get a look at my screen but I turned away from him.

"I'm getting an Uber."

"The hell you are." He tried to take the phone from me but I moved it out of his reach. "Nyla, you're *not* doing that. I brought you here, and I'm seeing you home."

"What part of *I'm a grown-ass woman* don't you seem to get, Cam??"

"Fine. Be grown, be mad at me, but I refuse to let you get in some stranger's car when I'm right here," he insisted, his voice strong. His eyes looked right into mine, making it clear he wasn't backing down on this one. "There's no way in hell."

"I'll call Kori, then."

"Come *on*! Look, I get it; I probably overreacted earlier. And if you want to bounce, I'll respect that. But let me make it up to you at least a little bit by getting you home safe. You can cuss me out or ignore me on the way. Just let me take you home myself, Nyla." His eyes softened again. "Please?"

There were a few '*awww*'s' around us and murmurs of how sweet that was. And some lady making it known she wouldn't mind Cam taking *her* home. Because, of course.

I glared at him, then sucked my teeth and turned towards the door. Cam followed me out.

"Wait here; I'll bring the car around," he instructed once we were on the sidewalk.

"Not necessary." I was already stomping towards his car. "Let's just go."

I heard him sigh from behind me, but he still rushed to beat me to the car so he could open the passenger door for me. I got into the car without looking at him, my arms tightly folded. As soon as he slid into the driver's seat, I turned to face the other direction, refusing to say anything else. Despite what he considered to be good intentions, he was still way out of line earlier. And for the time being, I was back to not having anything to say to him.

And he still didn't even notice this damn eyeliner.

Chapter 6

By the next day, I had cooled off considerably. Cam had sent a few texts since he dropped me off the night before, and I'd only given short replies. It was hard to stay *too* mad at him; I knew he only acted like that out of concern. He just needed to reel it in.

I thankfully had the apartment to myself, listening to some Donnell Jones while I made dinner. Salmon, green beans, roasted potatoes. I had just oiled and seasoned the beans and put them in the oven to roast when my phone started playing 'Best Friend' by Brandy.

"Cam," I sighed, wiping my hands on a dish towel. "I wish the men I dated were this persistent."

(Fun fact: my original ringtone for Cam was 'I Wanna Be Your Lover' by Prince, but knew I'd have to explain that if anyone other than Kori heard it).

"Hey," Cam greeted once I answered.

"Hey."

"I'm over your way; can I come by?"

"Jada isn't here."

"So?"

"She's the main reason you come over here lately."

He sighed. I wasn't trying to be snarky but I had to keep my guard up at least a little. Being upset with Cam was way easier than yearning for him. "Nyla."

"Fine, come on."

"Thank you."

He showed up about fifteen minutes later, when I was tossing lemon zest into the green beans.

"Smells good in here," he commented, entering the small kitchen.

"Thanks."

"Still mad at me?"

I moved over to take the salmon out of the air fryer. "Not really. Though you were still way out of line last night."

"I know," he admitted, coming over to lean against the counter next to me. My eyes were on the food but I could feel him watching. "When I thought about it later, I realized that, myself. I shouldn't have stepped to buddy like that."

"No, you shouldn't have. He seemed like a nice guy, plus he was cute. You totally blocked me."

"I'm not gonna act like I'm overly sorry about *that*; just how I went about it."

My hands fell to my sides as I turned to look at him. "That's ridiculous, Cam. What's up with the double standard? You can do what you want but I can't?"

"It's not that." He slid a little closer to me. "I don't know how to explain it, Nyla; I'm just overly protective of the people I love. And ever since that day on the sidewalk, I've wanted to protect you, probably more than anybody else."

"Why? Because you don't think I can take care of myself?"

"I know you can. But *I* want to take care of you, too. I know I can go overboard with it sometimes, but it's all out of love, Nyla. Please know that."

I fiddled with the edge of the plate in front of me, warning myself not to melt over his words. It wasn't that I doubted his sincerity; it was more about protecting *myself*.

"Are you like this with Jada?" I couldn't resist asking, my eyes on the counter. "You get this crazy over her?"

"Jada and I have our thing, but she's not you." He gently took my fiddling hand and brought it to his chest. "I only have one best friend, and I'm looking at her. And I hate when you're pissed at me so if I promise to take a deep breath and count to ten the next time I see someone trying to step to you, will you forgive me?"

Damn it. He was being such a sweetheart I couldn't help but smile up at him. It was hard to stay mad when he said this kind of stuff. Especially since I knew he wasn't just blowing smoke. I'd never known Cam to be a liar during the time I'd known him. Overzealous, oblivious, and a little narrow-minded, maybe, but not a liar.

"Next two movie nights are chick flicks," I told him with a smile, the hand that was encased in his giving his chest a little nudge. "Or documentaries."

"Damn. Really punishing me, huh? Fine." He winked at me, returning my smile. "I guess I deserve it."

"You do. But for the record, Cam, I *do* appreciate you wanting to look out for me so much. You need to know that. It might drive me crazy sometimes but I love you for it."

"I know you do. Come here."

He pulled me into a hug, his long legs on either side of me, and I rested my cheek against his chest with a sigh. I had to resist the urge to press my body into his groin. He just felt and smelled so good...

It crossed my mind again to tell him how I really felt about him, and for once, I didn't automatically try to talk myself out of it. Maybe it *wasn't* so crazy to think that Cam's feelings might match mine, or that he could start seeing me as more than a friend if he knew how I felt. The way he acted with P.J. the night before didn't seem like just aggressive concern for a friend. Maybe it was also a little, dare I say...jealousy?

I wasn't sure where this burst of confidence was coming from, but I wasn't going to waste it.

Lifting my head, I looked at his handsome face and nervously licked my lips. "Hey, Cam, can I ask you something?"

"Of course." He gently smoothed a lock of my short hair and grazed his curled fingers down my cheek, gently tweaking my chin. He dropped his eyes to mine, the smile still on his lips. His other hand still clamped me to him. "What's up?"

His eyes dipped to my cleavage for a second before snapping back up to my face. Did he just peek at my breasts?? My confidence (and ever-latent horniness) surged at the thought.

Even more emboldened, I stood a little straighter, easing closer to him a teensy-weensy bit. "Do you think that friends can...well...do you think it's possible that-"

"There you are."

We both looked over at Jada, who had just walked in. I didn't even hear the front door open. Her eyes were on Cam, then they dropped to his hand that was still locked on my waist. She glanced at me briefly before looking back at him. "I've been calling you."

"My phone was on vibrate," Cam replied as I eased away from him, going back to my plate. "My bad."

"I didn't know you were coming over here."

"Had to talk to Nyla."

"Hmm." She strolled over and took my vacated spot in front of him, pressing her body to his and giving him a kiss smack on the lips. "So I guess I interrupted."

Cam just grunted and leaned in for another kiss, muttering something about missing her. And I tried not to feel like I had just gotten kicked in the face.

"Um, I'll just leave you two alone," I muttered, picking up my plate and turning to leave.

"Why?" Cam immediately asked.

"Yeah, you don't have to go anywhere," Jada added. I noted the possessive way she leaned into Cam, and I'm sure she wanted me to notice. "We can all hang out. *Together*."

"And you were about to ask me something, right?" Cam confirmed.

"I was, but never mind. The answer actually just hit me. See you two later." I forced myself to flash them a smile before heading out of the kitchen and towards my bedroom, releasing a long shaky breath once I was behind the closed door. Thank goodness Jada came in when she did; I was likely about to make a huge fool out of myself.

I couldn't even enjoy my food; I just picked at it as I listened to Cam and Jada laughing in the living room. If I didn't know Cam better than that, I'd let the paranoid side of me think I was the subject of their amusement. Jada had a look in her eye just then that said she sensed I was up to something, and I figured things were only going to get even more tense between us. She already hadn't said that much to me since asking if something was going on between me and Cam. I didn't care because it wasn't like we were friends, anyway, but I couldn't help but wonder what she said about me to Cam when they were alone. She mentioned they had argued because of me. Oh, to be a fly on the wall.

Figuring I'd go ahead and get my work clothes together for the next day, I pulled some slacks and a blouse from my closet and was getting them ready to iron when I heard Cam call me from the living room.

"Ugh, *what*?" I muttered, seriously considering pretending to be asleep. I couldn't imagine Jada would have left us there alone again so I wondered what in the world Cam would be calling me out there for with her there.

After a quick check in the mirror, I yanked open my bedroom door and trudged to the living room. Sure enough, Jada was snuggled against Cam on the couch, her leg thrown over his and an arm draped across his stomach. She almost looked mischievous.

Or...taunting.

"Yeah?" I asked, my eyes on Cam.

"I was just talking to Jada and we have an idea."

My brow furrowed skeptically. "An idea about what?"

"How 'bout we fix you up?"

"Nope," I immediately retorted, shaking my head vehemently. "Absolutely not. No thank you."

"Aww, why not? I figured this would be a way to make up for what I did at the movies last night."

Jada looked back and forth between us. "You two went to the movies together?"

I resisted the urge to smirk at the revelation that Cam apparently hadn't told her that.

"Yeah," Cam answered distractedly. "And I kinda busted her game up when somebody tried to step to her. So I figured-"

"Wait, *that's* why we're doing this?" Jada marveled, sitting up and frowning at him. "I thought we were just helping her get a man 'cause she was so lonely."

Wow.

"Why does it matter? You're the one who suggested this in the first place. If I hadn't shown my ass like I did last night, I wouldn't even be agreeing to this shit."

"And why *wouldn't* you? You have a problem with Nyla being with somebody else??"

"I don't love it."

"Why??"

He hesitated, glancing at me. Cam didn't usually get flustered so I found it interesting that he couldn't find his words all of a sudden.

"Jada, I need you to chill out," he finally said to her, exasperated. "I'm not in the mood to argue with you."

"We're not arguing. I'm simply asking why it's such a problem for you if Nyla dates someone else. Why do you care so much about it?"

"Jada, Nyla is...she's special to me. I don't expect you to understand it."

"Well, *make* me understand it. If you two are *just* friends-"

"Um, hello?" I interjected, waving a hand. "Remember me? The person you're discussing? Y'all are really arguing for nothing because I don't want or need you to set me up. But thanks for the offer."

Cam threw up his hands. "Fine with me. It's not like you have to twist my arm to let it go."

Jada glared at Cam, and I sensed that he was going to be hearing more about this when they were alone. She looked at me and stretched her, as she's called them, better-than-Lauryn-Hill's lips into a condescending smile.

"Nyla, I wish I could be like you," she sneered, her voice taking on an overly sweet tone. "You're just so comfortable being by yourself. I personally prefer having a man to spending every night alone, but you clearly don't need that. Maybe one day you can get a cat or something."

I narrowed my eyes at her, and we shared a glare for several moments. Just like that, I didn't like her.

"Actually, Jada," I replied, putting on my own fake smile. "You clearly have the wrong idea about me. I'm not lonely at all. In fact, there's someone I'm quite taken with."

Her eyebrows shot up in surprise while Cam sat forward, looking at me with a frown.

"Who?" he barked.

"Don't worry about all that."

"Nyla, *who* are you talking about??"

"Damn, she said don't worry about it," Jada fussed at him, nudging his chest. "I still don't see why you get so upset about that."

Cam's eyes were still on me. "Nyla, do we need to talk?"

"No, Cam. I believe we already discussed this kind of thing earlier," I reminded, arching a brow. "Remember?"

His frown easing slightly, he sat back. I knew he didn't want to leave it at that but thankfully, he did.

"Yeah, well, whatever," Jada huffed, jumping to her feet. She grabbed Cam's hand. "Come on, let's go to my room and leave Nyla *alone*."

She shot me a look with that last word but I just shook my head at her. She still hadn't learned that my game face could be epic. I was great at holding it together in front of other people when I needed to.

I just chuckled to myself as Jada dragged Cam to her room, him giving me a look as they passed. As soon as they were gone, my smile faded and I rubbed the back of my neck.

This was getting to be a little much, this little awkward threesome that Cam, Jada and I had going on. It would've been much easier if I *did* actually have someone to spend time with, so I wasn't always in third wheel territory. But unfortunately, there were no real prospects on the horizon.

At least I didn't lie; I *was* quite taken with someone. And I wonder what would've happened if I'd blurted out that it was Cam to both of them. The reactions almost would have been worth whatever would've come after that.

I went back to my room to get my barely-touched dinner and put it away in the kitchen, figuring I could just have it the next day. After quickly cleaning up the dishes, I started to head back to my room when there was a knock on the door.

Frowning curiously, I went over and checked the peephole.

"Good grief," I muttered, shaking my head. I opened the door with a hand on my hip. "What are you doing over here, Kendrick? Why didn't you call first?"

"I *did* call. Three times; you never answered."

Remembering I'd left my phone in my room while I was having that pointless conversation with Cam and Jada, I figured that must've been when he called. "Well, I'm sorry I missed it but why did you come, anyway?"

He stood there, filling up my doorway, looking at me intently. There were flowers clutched in his fist. "I needed to see you and I figured I wouldn't be able to get you to come over to my spot. Especially since you turned down the pork chops last time I invited you. If you won't come for those, you won't come for anything."

My lips quivered, trying to hold in the smile but it didn't quite work. I just chuckled behind my hand and stepped aside, opening the door wider. "Come on in here."

He stepped inside, and the room immediately looked smaller. Sometimes I forgot just how big Kendrick was. But then, most people looked big compared to me.

"I got you these," he announced, holding out the bouquet of tulips. "Your favorite, right?"

I eyed him for a moment before taking the flowers. "My favorites are actually carnations...but I still appreciate it. These are beautiful, thank you."

"Damn, my bad." He shook his head, cursing under his breath. "I'm already messing this up..."

"Messing what up? What's going on?"

"I'm not just bringing you these for the hell of it," he revealed.

"Okay..."

Standing up a little taller, he reached for my free hand and looked into my eyes, his expression serious. "Nyla, I've been thinking a lot about us lately. And the more I *do* think about it, the more I want us to try again."

My jaw dropped. "Are you serious?"

"Dead serious. I want us to get back together."

"Kendrick..." I gently slid my hand from his and moved past him to the kitchen. He was right on my heels and eyed me as I got a vase from under the cabinet. "I don't think that's a good idea. We broke up for a reason."

"Yeah, but that was then and this is now," he retorted, coming over to stand next to me as I filled the vase with water and slid the flowers inside. "It's been a couple of years. We've both matured since then, right?"

"I mean, yeah...but still." I retreated back to the living room and again, he followed me. Taking my time putting the vase on the end table and rearranging a few of the flowers, I finally turned back to him. "Just because some time has passed doesn't mean we need to try a relationship again."

"I disagree. It took that time apart for me to really appreciate you. I admit I didn't before; not like I should have. But I know what it's like to lose you now. And I'm willing to do whatever's necessary so I won't let that happen again."

"Oh, Kendrick..." I couldn't deny how sweet that was. "That's...that's *so* nice. And I'm sure you mean it. But-"

"I just want a shot," Kendrick insisted, stepping over to grab my hands. His dark eyes looked almost pleading. "You have no idea how much I've been missing you, and kicking myself for not being the man you needed and deserved. Before you shoot me down, *at least* tell me you'll think about it."

"Kendrick-"

He pulled me to him, leaning down to press his lips against mine. Literally lifting me off my feet, he gently eased my lips open with his tongue, and despite my spoken reservations, I found myself returning his kiss. My arms slowly slid around his neck as we exchanged slow, exploratory kisses, almost as if we were testing each other out again. As I usually did with Kendrick, I let myself get caught up in the moment, moaning slightly as I closed my eyes and enjoyed it.

"Well, this is interesting..."

"What the hell??"

Jada and Cam's simultaneous voices jarred me out of my momentary enjoyment. I jumped, looking over at them in alarm before gazing at Kendrick as if I didn't know how I got several inches off the floor and into his arms.

"What's going on?" Cam demanded before catching himself. Jada shot him a look but he barely glanced at her; he was focused on me and Kendrick. "I mean...I, uh...we didn't know you had company, Nyla."

"Uh, yeah." Remembering that I was still hoisted off the ground, I patted Kendrick's shoulders, signaling for him to put me down. He did, though reluctantly. "You remember Kendrick. Oh, and this is Jada," I informed Kendrick, throwing a hand in her direction. "My roommate."

"I'm also Cam's girlfriend," Jada added pointedly.

"Nice meeting you." Kendrick nodded to her before turning his attention back to me. I noticed he didn't acknowledge Cam and Cam must have, too, considering how he was glaring at him. But he did that with any man that showed me attention, so who knew.

"So I guess you *weren't* kidding when you said there was somebody you were into," Jada said to me. Her smile almost looked relieved. "I thought you were just saying that because you didn't want us to set you up."

"Nope," I replied, though my face was tightening. I didn't want Kendrick to get the wrong idea, thinking I was harboring some feelings for him that I wasn't. "Meant everything I said."

I could feel Kendrick looking at me but I kept my eyes on Jada, while Cam kept his glare aimed at Kendrick.

"You've been talking about me, huh?" Kendrick asked me, smiling smugly.

"Don't...go reading too much into that," I muttered, cutting my eyes in his direction.

"You apparently said you were feeling somebody and with the way you were kissing me just now-"

"Kendrick, can we wait to talk about this when we're alone, please?"

"So you two are back together?" Cam asked, looking right at me. "I didn't, uh...I didn't know you were considering that, Nyla."

"We're *not* back together."

"Yet," Kendrick added, winking at me.

"Oh god..." I groaned, rubbing my hands down my face.

This is what I got for feeling the need to blurt out that I was into someone just because Jada was trying to push my buttons. It just figured that Kendrick would show up right after that, and I'd let myself end up kissing him, and Cam and Jada would *catch* us kissing. I mean, who would've thought? Kori would probably find all of this hilarious.

"Come on, baby, let's leave them alone," Jada said to Cam, grabbing his arm. "I haven't eaten since lunch, so you can feed me and Nyla can have some privacy with her man."

"*Not* my man," I reminded from behind my hands.

"Yet."

"Kendrick!"

"Let's go, Cam," Jada grinned at me, pulling Cam along with her as she moved towards the door. I peeked between my fingers to see Cam wordlessly going along with her, giving me a pained look.

Chapter 7

I really needed to learn to keep my mouth shut.

Thanks to my big mouth, Kendrick was calling me ten times a day and Cam was bugging me for details about a relationship I wasn't even in.

Between all of that, I still hadn't really taken time to process the reason for Kendrick's visit in the first place. It wasn't the first time he'd suggested we get back together, but it was definitely the time I took him most seriously. He'd never humbled himself like that, admitting his part in things. Usually he tried to put it all on me or try things like getting me to talk to his mother so they could double-team me. I was honestly touched, even if I still didn't think us trying again was the thing to do.

Of course, Kori thought I should just bite the bullet and tell Cam the real deal. And maybe doing that *would* stop the bleeding. But every time I told myself to just go ahead and do it, I remembered him kissing Jada right in my face. And despite how close we were, we really hadn't talked much at all about his relationship with her; I had no idea how deep his feelings for her went. If this was just a fling for him or something he felt could go the distance. I'd like to think if it was the latter, he would have said that to me by then. And Jada seemed more about fun than forever.

So I told myself to just hang on until things between him and Jada fizzled out.

In the meantime, I still had to deal with Kendrick. He thought I was just trying to be coy when I tried to (gently) tell him that we needed to pump the brakes on this whole getting back together thing.

"Kendrick, I don't know how many more ways I can say this," I said to him when I finally answered one of his calls. "While I appreciate the gesture, I was serious when I said we just need to keep things as they are."

"Then why did you kiss me the way you did?"

"Kendrick, *I* didn't kiss *you*. I just didn't stop it when *you* kissed *me*. There's a difference."

"And what about when you jumped me at my place a while back? I didn't start anything that time. That was all you."

"Yes, I'm aware..."

"I mean, if you're not feeling me at all, why are you acting like you do? You playing games? I never thought you were a tease, Nyla."

"I'm not...Kendrick, I'm sorry if I gave you that impression. I'm seriously not trying to send you mixed signals."

"Then what *are* you doing?"

"I don't know," I sighed. "Clearly, I'm kinda all over the place. And it's not fair to you."

"Nyla, if this is you trying some new way to brush me off, I'm not falling for it," he said strongly. "Especially since you still haven't said who it was you were talking about when you told your roommate that you had a new man."

"That's not what I told her. All I said was that I was taken with somebody. And I really only said that to shut her up."

"I still say we can work as a couple this time if you'd just quit thinking about how I was back then and focus on how I am now," he insisted. "People can change."

"I know that, Kendrick. How 'bout you just...let me think about all this, okay? Give me a little time to sort everything out."

He paused for a few moments before responding. "All right. Take whatever time you need."

It was one of those days at work when I had meeting after meeting and was expected to be alert in all of them. But by the third one, it almost felt like a punishment. Endless talks about metrics was making my mind go numb.

My attention started slipping, and to keep myself awake, I went to the vault of scenarios I had cooked up over the time I'd known Cam that almost always made me feel better. There were quite a few...Cam and I playing in the ocean before he kisses me passionately at sunset; him waking me up by sliding his body on top of mine; us dining at a nice restaurant and him surprising me with a serenade and a declaration of love in front of everyone; Cam and I at the altar. There were others but these were the top tier ones. And regardless of their apparent improbability of actually coming true, it still brought me pleasure to think about them.

Unfortunately, I was enjoying them a little *too* much this time. Fantasy Cam had just ripped off his shirt and lifted my legs around his waist on the crisp white sheets of a hotel room bed when someone nudged my arm.

"They're talking to you," Maria, one of the other supervisors, murmured to me.

"Huh? What?" I looked at her, then at our manager Zack, who was standing at the head of the table eying me curiously, along with everyone else. "I'm sorry, what did you say?"

"You sure are smiling a lot today," he observed. His boy band-looking hair fell across his face. "I guess you're pretty excited about the new position that's opening up, huh?"

"Oh...uh, yeah," I stammered, not wanting to admit I had no clue what he was talking about. "I guess you could say that."

"I've been meaning to ask if you were going to go for it. You're certainly qualified to take over once I leave in a couple of months."

Wow, I really *hadn't* been paying any attention; I didn't even know Zack would be leaving.

"Well, you know," I cleared my throat and sat up a little straighter in my seat, "I figured it couldn't hurt to give it a shot, right? Worst that can happen is I get turned down."

"That's a great attitude. Good luck to you, Nyla. I think you'd do a great job."

"Thanks, Zack."

Once the meeting was finally over, I meandered back to my desk, thinking about what I had just mindlessly agreed to. I hadn't thought about trying for a promotion in a while; I wasn't even sure I *wanted* to be a manager. It was so much more headache for not all that much more pay.

But then I realized that if I were to get the position, I likely wouldn't need a roommate anymore. So that was enough to make me consider it right there.

But *then* I realized that if Jada moved out of *my* place, she might end up at Cam's. So I was back to the drawing board as far as whether to bother or not.

I'd only been back at my desk about twenty minutes when I heard a knock on the edge of my cubicle. At least if I was a manager, I'd get an actual office.

"Hey, Nyla?"

I turned to see Leslie standing there with a nervous smile.

"Leslie, hey. What's up?"

"I've been meaning to thank you," she said, easing inside the cubicle and leaning a hip on my desk. Her voice lowered. "For not ratting me out about...you know."

"Oh, that. Don't mention it." Truth be told, I hadn't given second thought to catching her getting some midday delight in the bathroom. If anything, I thought it was funny.

"I want to let you know how much I appreciate it, though, because most people around here wouldn't have hesitated to call me out," she continued, leaning towards me and lowering her voice even more. "Or at least gossiped about it to somebody. I'm sure you know how people talk in this office. But I haven't heard anything about it, so I can only imagine you kept it to yourself."

"Haven't told a soul." Well, I *did* mention it to Kori eventually, but she didn't work there anymore so that didn't count, as far as I was concerned.

"Thank you for that, for real. I don't want something like that coming into play when it comes time for me to try to move up around here. You know I have a five-year timeline."

"I didn't, but that's great. It's good to have a plan."

"Speaking of moving up, I hear you might be taking over Zack's position when he leaves."

Damn, word spread fast. I was almost sure Leslie hadn't been in that meeting just now so I didn't know how in the world she heard about that already.

"I'm thinking about it," I replied, noncommittal. "Weighing pros and cons, and all that."

"I get it. Well just know that I'm going to be hyping you up as much as I can, whether you decide to go for that or not. I've already sent a Star Acknowledgement to Zack about you."

"Wow, really?" A Star Acknowledgment was positive feedback or reviews employees could send about each other, and they were posted on the internal company portal. At the end of the quarter, the person with the most acknowledgments won a prize, usually their choice of gift cards or some kind of home item. The last person that won couldn't stop bragging about their top-of-the-line robot vacuum.

"Well, thank you for that, Leslie, but you really didn't have to do that just because I didn't tell your business."

"Please, Nyla, you and I both know how rare that is around here. If it was anyone else that caught me and Leo, this whole floor would've known about it within the hour."

True.

"So it's nice to know there's someone around here I can trust," she continued. "Hey, you wanna have lunch today?"

"Uh, sure, we can."

"Great!" She skipped away from my desk.

I just shook my head and got back to work.

"Kori, I've never had so many people confide in me in my *life*!" I exclaimed to her a couple of days later. "Ever since Leslie apparently made it known that I was good at keeping secrets, everybody wants to tell me their personal business!"

Kori laughed loudly, as she had been the entire time I'd been telling this story. Starting from how Leslie confided in me about something she really only needed to be telling her gynecologist. Kinda ruined my lunch with that.

"Well, we all know you're good at keeping secrets, girl," Kori said, kicking her bare feet up on her couch. She'd just gotten home after a long day so I offered to bring her dinner. "Look how long you've been keeping quiet about how you really feel about Cam."

"Do we have to talk about that *every* time we hang out?"

"Until you do something about it, yes."

"Kori, come on; there's nothing for me to do. He's with Jada. You know this."

"And now you've gone and complicated things by letting Kendrick back in the picture."

"He's not. Not really."

"*He* thinks he is. And you're not helping things by kissing on him every time he comes around."

"I know. I don't even know why I do that."

"Loneliness? Spite? Consolation prize?"

"Not that last one. I wouldn't use him like that. Not on purpose, anyway."

"Do you want him back?"

"I...I'm not sure. I mean, there has to be a reason I don't just wash my hands of him completely. It's not like I keep entertaining any of my other exes like this."

"I like Kendrick all right; maybe he *has* matured since the two of you were together. It's possible. But just be sure that you're not just using him as a way to get over Cam, or to try to teach him some kind of lesson. That almost never works."

"I wouldn't do that. But it might be a moot point anyway since I've been thinking about changing things up with my friendship with Cam."

Kori paused her action of opening the Chinese takeout containers. "Changing things up how?"

"By ending it."

"What??" She dropped her hands and turned to me. "Why would you want to do that, Nyla?"

"Because...it's getting too hard to be around him. Him being so protective over me and the occasional moments where I delude myself into thinking that his feelings for me are at least a little romantic, and then in the next breath he's kissing on my roommate. And Jada seems to take enjoyment out of it; it's like she senses that I'm feeling him and is rubbing it in that she has him and I don't. I guess she's getting me back for not letting her vacuum in the buff."

"She does that?"

"Naked housework, naked yoga, naked dance parties. She really likes being naked. No wonder Cam is so googly-eyed."

Kori shook her head. "So instead of just telling him how you feel and letting the chips fall where they may, you'd rather end your friendship altogether?"

"Maybe that's better in the long run," I replied, trying to convince myself. "Maybe Cam came into my life for a season and...now that season is ending."

"You don't even believe that, Nyla, and you know it." She slid the eggrolls over to me, giving me a stern look. "You're making this harder on yourself than you need to. Just tell him."

"'Just tell him.' Like it's the easiest thing to confess your love for someone without having *any* idea that they feel the same way about you. I wish you'd recognize that, Kori."

"So you're worried about being embarrassed? Honey, it happens. Who *hasn't* been embarrassed over a man at some point or another?"

"As clumsy as I am, I've been embarrassed plenty. I'm worried about getting hurt."

"You're already hurt. Him getting with Jada in the first place hurt. Every time you hear them banging in the next room hurts."

"Is this supposed to be making me feel better?"

"This is supposed to wake you up and stop you from throwing away something you know you're not ready to throw away. If you ended your friendship with Cam, you'd be miserable." She nudged my arm, waiting for me to look at her. When I did, she continued. "And regardless of what kind of love it is, Cam has a lot of it for you. Don't do that to him without at least giving him the truth about why."

She had a point. Even if it wasn't the kind of love I dreamed and fantasized about, Cam *did* love me. He proved it with his actions. And if I was honest with myself, I didn't want him out of my life.

But I was also honestly scared to death of confessing my feelings to him. Of asking him to leave Jada and come to me. I wasn't usually bashful, but being in love with my best friend was something different.

And I knew that if I told him I was in love with him and he just gave me some kind of polite platitude with a pat on the head and went back to Jada, there'd be no coming back from it. Even if our friendship continued, it wouldn't be the same. So it was either continue to yearn or end it.

Either way, I lost.

Chapter 8

"Hey Nyla, I need to ask you something. Whoa!"

Cam reached out and grabbed me before I hit the ground. I'd somehow managed to trip over nothing.

"You all right?" he asked, his arm still around my waist.

"Yeah, I'm fine." I eased away from his touch, even though I wanted to linger a few more seconds. I raked my fingers through my short hair. "What did you want to ask me?"

We were cruising through the farmers market, which he had somehow talked me into. I swear I hated how he was able to sway me sometimes, because I had initially declined when he invited me. I wasn't super pumped to watch him buy the ingredients for some romantic dinner for Jada, even though he hadn't said that's what he was shopping for. But that's what it was for in my imagination.

"Is Jada seeing anybody else?"

"What?"

"Is she cheating on me?"

"Oh, Cam, don't ask me this kind of stuff. I don't want to get involved in your relationship."

"So she *is*."

"I honestly have no idea. You know Jada and I aren't close like that. She doesn't tell me her business."

"And you haven't heard her talking to somebody else, or..."

"Why are you asking, Cam?"

"I just have a feeling something is going on." He mindlessly perused the display of peaches. "Nothing in particular has happened; you know how you just get a gut feeling?"

"I suppose. You should ask her about it, if you're suspicious."

"You really think she'd tell me the truth if she was messing around?"

"She might." I shrugged. "Some people are unabashedly honest like that."

"Not Jada," he muttered.

I glanced at him curiously. His jaw was clenched. Now I couldn't help but wonder what was going on between them. Jada hadn't been acting any differently, from what I noticed. Was there trouble in paradise already?

"Are you two even exclusive?" I asked him. "If it's just sex, then..."

"Is that what it is between you and your boy?"

"Who?"

"You know who, Nyla."

"Kendrick? Why? And way to change the subject, by the way."

"I've been meaning to ask you for a while. Ever since I caught y'all grinding in the middle of the living room."

"We were not."

"He picked you up, Nyla. Was standing there hoisting you up like a sack of groceries."

"He's over a foot taller than me, Cam. It was either that or I stand on something."

"And his hands were on your ass!"

"You probably don't wanna know where mine were the last time I was at his place."

He stopped and glared at me. "You trying to be funny?"

"Cam, what is the big deal?" I was actually amused by this for once. "Am I supposed to be a nun while you get to have all the sex?"

"So y'all *are* having sex!!"

"Cam!" I nudged him and looked over at the intrigued fruit vendor, who didn't even try to act like he wasn't listening. Grabbing Cam's arm, I hurried further away from listening ears. "I really need you to chill out. Do you not like Kendrick? Well, you probably don't, since you automatically seem to hate any man that shows interest in me."

He just stood there looking at me thoughtfully for a few moments, trying to gather his words. Then he stepped closer.

"You've been different recently, Nyla," he informed, his brow furrowed. There was no trace of amusement in his expression. "I don't know if it's because of this dude or something else, but things haven't been the same with us. And I think you know that."

"And you think it's because of Kendrick?"

"It's because of *something*. And I don't like it."

I'm in love with you. And I know you don't feel the same way about me. It's getting harder to handle, especially with seeing you with someone else, so I've been pulling away.

I forced myself to hold his eye contact. The truth was on the tip of my tongue, and I tried to force myself to push it over the edge and out of my mouth. I could practically hear Kori's voice in my head, urging me to just say it.

Why couldn't I just say it??

"Things change, Cam," is what I finally said, my voice cracking a little. "Not everything – or every relationship – stays the same forever."

He stepped closer to me. "What are you saying?"

My mouth opened but nothing came out at first. "I..."

"You're not talking about you and me, are you?" His eyes searched mine. "Tell me what you mean, Nyla."

"What if...what if things *did* change between us?" I hedged. Maybe I could slow-walk into admission. "Would that be such a bad thing? Some changes are good..."

"I don't *want* anything to change between us. You mean a lot to me, Nyla. And I get that you're going to eventually fall for someone and do your own thing, but - and maybe this is selfish of me - I hope you'll still find time and space for me in your life *somewhere*."

"Why?"

"What do you mean, why? You *know* I love you."

"Cam..." My eyes were wet and I had to look away. "I love you, too. But if you hadn't saved me on the street that day, your life wouldn't be any different."

"No," he immediately protested, shaking his head. "I disagree. My life is better for having you in it. There's not a doubt in my mind about that. I wish you would believe me when I tell you how much you mean to me, Nyla. I'm not bullshitting when I tell you that."

"It's not that I don't believe you, Cam, it's just..." I briefly covered my face with my hands, taking a step away from him. "Maybe I feel like I don't have a place in *your* life anymore, now that you're with Jada. And I know what you've said, but...I don't know. I'm just stepping back and letting you do your thing."

"Well, I don't need you to do that, so take a step back over this way." He gently grabbed my wrist and pulled me back to him. "I don't wanna lose you, whether I'm with Jada or anybody else. Get it in your head that you're locked in here, all right?"

My eyes dropped to where he was tapping over his heart. "I see."

"Friends like you are hard to come by." He slid an arm around my shoulders and kissed my forehead. "How we are now is how I want things to stay."

"Right. I get it."

He led me back over to the fruit tables, and I tried to regain some of my composure. Thank god I hadn't told him just how deep my love for him went. I needed to stop fooling myself. If I didn't know before, I knew now; this was all Cam and I would ever be. He said so himself. And I just needed to accept that and get over it.

"Hey, Kendrick."

"Is it okay to call you? I know you said you needed some time and all..."

"It's okay. What's up?"

"I wanted to see if you could hang out tonight. We could go to dinner or do something else; whatever you want."

"Umm..." I tapped my fingers on the steering wheel. I was still in the parking lot at work, having just left the office. "I'm not sure if that's the best idea right now..."

"It's just dinner."

"That's what you say, but the last couple of times we were around each other, it got physical."

"So? Look, Nyla, there's clearly something still between us. I'm willing to leave the past in the past and start over."

"Not trying to be a bitch or anything, Kendrick, but it's easy for you to say that considering you weren't the one that was unhappy. Towards the end, you were driving me crazy."

"That was *then*, though. I told you I've changed."

"How do I know that, though?"

"You *won't* know it until you give me a chance to prove it to you. I'm not making you a bunch of big promises, acting like I'm gonna be perfect 'cause I'm not. I just know I miss you. And I wanna see you tonight."

There was something endearing about that. Once upon a time, Kendrick would have told me whatever he thought I wanted to hear to get me to agree to what he asked. He'd have made grand promise after grand promise, telling me he'd move heaven and earth and get my hopes all up, and then would have nothing for me but excuses when he didn't back it up. I actually appreciated him keeping it to just wanting to see me for dinner instead of something crazy like talking about us getting engaged in a month.

"Well...you *did* promise me some pork chops," I reminded him, smiling.

"You're right, I did." I could tell he was smiling, too. "I was gonna take you out but I'll gladly hook you up with some of my prize-winning pork chops."

"What prize did they win, Kendrick?"

"First thing to run out at the family reunion. Enough said."

I laughed. "Silly. All right, umm...around seven?"

"Seven is good. Want me to come pick you up?"

"That's okay; I can just drive there. Thanks, though."

"See you tonight, Nyla."

I still wasn't sure seeing Kendrick was smart. Truth be told, I hadn't spent much time considering the possibility of another relationship with him. My mind had been so consumed with Cam that Kendrick had been pushed to the backburner.

But now that Cam had made it clear that all he and I were ever going to be was friends, now was as good a time as any to explore.

Thankfully Jada wasn't home when I got there, and I got showered and changed before heading over to Kendrick's. My phone chimed with a text from Cam as I was heading down the stairs from my apartment, and I almost rolled my ankle trying to read it. I tried not to think of it as a sign that dealing with Cam only led to pain for me and instead just admitted that my clumsy ass I didn't need to be trying to walk and read at the same time, especially going down some stairs.

I was actually a little nervous when I arrived at Kendrick's. Taking a deep breath, I reminded myself to be present, and keep thoughts of everything and everyone else out of my mind while I was there. If I wasn't going to give this a fair shot, I was just wasting both of our time.

"Hey," Kendrick smiled after I finally made myself knock on the door. "Come on in."

"Hey." Smiling tightly, I stepped inside and was immediately assaulted with the aromas from his kitchen. If Kendrick couldn't do anything else, he could cook. "Oh my gosh, that smells *amazing*, Kendrick."

"Thank you kindly. I'm doing something new; these are thick-cut chops with sausage and cornbread stuffing."

"Kendrick, I'm *not* gonna propose to you, no matter how much you entice me with deliciousness."

He threw his head back and laughed. "I can keep hope alive. But for now, I just want us to have a nice night together. How 'bout that?"

I felt my smile relax. "That sounds good."

"Good. Take your shoes off; get comfortable. The food will be ready in a few minutes. You want some wine?"

"Um, just some juice or water is fine."

"I got you."

My tension steadily melted away as I hung out in the kitchen with Kendrick as he finished dinner. He told me about the latest tales of the football team he coached, and I shared how I'd unwillingly become everyone's personal therapist at work. By the time we sat down to eat, I felt lighter than I had in a while.

"It's good to see you laugh so much," he told me, taking a sip of his Corona. "Your smile is too pretty not to show it off more."

"I appreciate the compliment. And it *does* feel good to laugh."

"I'm glad I can be a part of what's making you feel good again. Even if that means bribing you with food."

Giggling, I cut another piece of my pork chop (which might've been my second one) and stuffed it into my mouth. "With food this good, I not that mad at it."

We finished gorging on his stuffed pork chops, sautéed greens, and mashed sweet potatoes and moved over to the living room, still laughing amongst ourselves. He turned on some music and I felt myself relax even more.

"You wanna play some cards?" he asked me.

"We can. Ooh, do you still have those board games? That would be fun."

"Oh yeah; they're back there in the closet. I'll go get 'em."

So we sat on the floor of his living room playing Monopoly and Scrabble, joking around with each other and having probably the best time we'd had together in years. I didn't think about Cam at all, which was a great sign. If tonight was any indication of how things could be with Kendrick this time around, then maybe us trying again might not be a bad idea.

"I'll be right back," I said, standing. After a quick bathroom break, I started to head back to the living room when I stopped at the ajar door of Kendrick's bedroom. I just stood there, gazing at his freshly-vacuumed carpet, floor-length emerald green curtains...king-sized bed. For some reason my eyes stuck to that, and I remembered how long it'd been since I'd gotten any. *Too* long.

I guess I was standing there longer than I realized because before I knew it, Kendrick was behind me, sliding his hands around my waist.

"I was wondering what happened to you," he said in my ear, his voice low.

"I'm sorry. I don't even know why I stopped right here."

"Wanna go in?" I felt his body press a little closer to mine.

It was on my lips to say no. But I turned in his arms and placed my hands on his chest. "I kinda do."

He leaned down and kissed me, and my arms slid up around his neck. I briefly questioned whether I should've been doing this as he started to slowly walk me backwards into the room. His hands slid down my butt to the back of my thighs, lifting me. Then we were both on the bed, me on his lap, making out with steadily increasing intensity.

"Damn, I missed you," he whispered between kisses. "You sure you're good with this?"

"Yes," I panted, drawing a sharp intake of breath when his hand palmed my breast. "Yes, I'm sure."

No more words needed to be said. Kendrick ripped my shirt off, then his.

Sex with Kendrick was...nice. It was nice when we were together before, and it was nice now. But that's *all* it was. Nothing mind-blowing. No toes being curled. We didn't even talk that much. It was quiet, sweaty, breathy sex. Which wouldn't have been so bad if I didn't know that's how it *always* was with Kendrick.

I guess not *everything* about him had changed.

He was half-asleep when I eased out of his bed to get dressed. It was after midnight and I didn't want to still be there later in the morning and have to have an awkward conversation about anything. I just needed to go home and process this whole night.

I certainly wasn't expecting to see Jada getting out of some man's car when I pulled up. And it sure wasn't Cam's.

"Oh, uh...Nyla," Jada stammered when she saw me approaching from my car. "It's kinda late for you to be out during the week, isn't it?"

Shrugging, I just looked at her, not interested in her obvious deflection attempts.

"Were you with Cam?"

"I was not. And you clearly weren't, either."

"Look, it's not what you think," she finally said in a huff. "That guy that dropped me off...he's just a friend."

"You don't have to explain anything to me." I continued on towards the stairs leading to our apartment, Cam's questions about Jada's faithfulness ringing in my head.

"You're gonna tell Cam, aren't you?" she asked hurriedly, right on my heels.

"It's none of my business, Jada."

"Well, in case you change your mind, I'm asking that you keep this to yourself." Jada followed me inside after I got the door unlocked, watching me as I removed my jacket and sent a quick text to Kendrick letting him know I made it home safely. "Don't tell Cam, all right? We're arguing enough these days as it is."

Y'all have been doing that your entire relationship, from what I hear.

"Like I said, not my business."

"You promise?"

Rolling my eyes, I turned to her. "If it's nothing like you said, why are you putting so much energy into keeping it from him?"

She started to respond, then hesitated. While she stood there trying to get her words together, I went on to my bedroom, kinda wishing I'd stayed at Kendrick's.

Chapter 9

My already-aloof relationship with Jada became even more strained after I caught her getting out of another man's car late at night. It very well could have been nothing like she said, but she was acting awfully guilty for that to be the case.

Personally, I didn't care what Jada did. What I was concerned about was how it was going to affect Cam. I still didn't know how deep his feelings ran for her. Made me again wonder what it meant that he never talked about that.

After a few days of tiptoeing around each other (well, her tiptoeing around *me*), Jada finally cornered me when I got home from work.

"You got a minute?" she asked.

I took my time stashing my purse and things in my room. "Depends."

"On what?"

"On whether or not this is more accusations or ridiculous questions about me and Cam. Or some kind of confession that will put me in a difficult position. Because if it's any of that, I in fact do *not* have a minute."

"It's not that." Jada paused. "Well, not really."

"Then I *really* don't have a minute. And my friend Kori is coming by in a little bit, anyway."

"Nyla," she whined. "Come on, this is important. And I need to talk to somebody."

"And you chose *me*? I'm sure you have other friends you can confide in."

"Yeah, but none of them know Cam like you know him. And I need your input."

"Jada, this is gonna sound really, really mean, but I see I need to just say this flat-out: I do not care about you and Cam's relationship. Please stop trying to involve me in y'all's crap."

"Why are you so snippy? You have a bad day at work or something?"

"No."

"Then why are you-"

"Oh gosh, I *just* told you the reason!"

"Nyla." Jada looked at me with pleading eyes. "I get that we're not close like that and I haven't been the best roommate, but I'm asking you for this favor. I really need to get this off my chest and it's not something I can tell Cam, at least not yet. Can you please just sit down and listen?"

Letting my head fall back with a sigh, I relented and trudged back over to the couch. She smiled gratefully and joined me, noticing when I glanced at my watch. I could only hope she took the hint.

"Things aren't...great between me and Cam," she announced, rubbing her hands on her knees. "It's been really rocky with us lately."

"That's too bad."

"I'm just not sure where our relationship is going. We never really talk about it. Every time I try to bring it up he just tries to distract me with sex. And I admit, it usually works."

"Ugh..."

"But the fact that he never wants to talk about us or our future can't be a good thing, right? We've been dating for a little while now. I'd like to think he knows whether he wants this to go somewhere or not."

"Mm-hmm."

"I just wish I knew if I was wasting my time." Jada flopped against the back of the couch. "I don't wanna keep messing with Cam if this is all we're gonna do."

"Hmm."

"And I know what you're probably thinking, but just to set the record straight, I have not cheated on Cam. That man that dropped me off the other night was just a friend from college that I hang out with sometimes."

"Yeah."

She sighed, dropping her hands. "Are you gonna give any actual feedback, here?"

"Wasn't planning on it."

"Nyla!"

"What? I told you I didn't want to talk about this stuff in the first place."

"Well, we *are* talking about it. So you might as well participate."

"Uh, *no*...why don't you call your hang-out buddy 'cause I can always just get up and go on about my business. I agreed to listen, not respond."

"Then what's the point??"

"Exactly my thought."

"Nyla..."

"What is it you want me to say, Jada? To tell you to dump Cam? Encourage you to stick it out? Or are you hoping he's told me something that would give you some answers? Even if he did, I wouldn't broadcast it. So I really don't have anything for you."

"That's great, Nyla. I humble myself and come to you for advice and you've got nothing to give me. I'm sitting here telling you what I'm going through for nothing."

"No, no, that's not fair," I quickly retorted, holding up a finger. "In my defense, I told you up front that I didn't care."

She sucked her teeth. "I guess I shouldn't be surprised that you're being so difficult. Why *would* you want to help me out when you're so jealous of me?"

"Oh, so we're trying *that* now, huh? Okay, fine; I've got a few minutes before *Property Brothers* comes on. Why would I be jealous of you, Jada?"

"Because I have a man whose all over me and you haven't had anything serious since I've moved in here. You already said that football player-looking guy that was here that night wasn't your man. So maybe you just resent that I'm getting some and you're not."

"Nah, that's not it."

"Yes, it is. Why else would you always be so bitter? And don't think I haven't noticed that your whole attitude towards me changed once Cam and I got together. You resent me for being with Cam."

Another time I was grateful for my game face. My expression didn't budge even though it felt like I'd been hit with a splash of cold water.

"For one, I'm not bitter," I assured her. "I already told you I didn't have high hopes for you and Cam. 'Crash and burn', remember? You thought it was *so* funny when I said it but looks like I'm not too far off."

Her face tightened.

"And two, you're just trying to project your frustration about you and Cam onto me. *Cam* is the one you need to be talking to about all of this; I'm sure you could get him talking if you really tried. But maybe you're afraid he won't tell you what you want to hear. So you *let* him keep distracting you with dick so neither one of you has to acknowledge what you both probably already know."

I might've said more than I initially intended, but I had time. She wanted to push my buttons, so these are the truth treats that came out.

"So I guess you think you know all about this, huh?" She stood, towering over me with a hard frown. "You've got it *so* together that you can just tell me about myself, right?"

"Hey, *you* came to *me* for advice, Jada," I reminded her, standing also. "Don't try to get in your feelings because I didn't tell you what you wanted to hear."

"I don't need you to tell me *anything* about me and my man!"

"Clearly you do. And regardless of how upset you are, Jada, you're not gonna keep raising your voice to me in my space."

"Oh, now you're trying to tell me what to do?"

She took a step closer and I arched a brow, daring her to do something crazy. My being short didn't make me timid. If she thought she was going to intimidate me, she had another thing coming.

"Not sure what it is you think you're trying to do right now, but you need to rethink it," I warned.

She looked surprised for a second, then chuckled. "That's cute. What in the world do you think you're gonna do to me?"

"Nobody's trying to fight you, Jada. You're the one acting like you wanna jump. And I'm just telling you, if you *do*, you might not get the result you think you will. Take that however you want."

"Oh really?"

"What the hell is going on??"

I hadn't even heard Kori come in, but there she was, glaring at Jada. She quickly walked over and stood near me.

"How did *you* get in here??" Jada demanded.

"I have a key. And I hope you don't think you're about to do something to my friend right now 'cause I'll put a stop to *all* of that."

"What, now it's a double-team?" Jada shook her head, then turned her eyes to me. "All I wanted to do was talk to you about Cam, Nyla, and you turned it into something it didn't even have to be."

I shook my head. "No, that was you, Jada. Because I didn't cater to you like you're clearly used to, you threw a tantrum. *You* turned it into something it didn't have to be."

She narrowed her eyes and didn't respond for a few moments. "Maybe this doesn't work, us being together in the same space. Maybe I need to find somewhere else to live."

My affirmative nod was immediate. "Maybe you should."

Without another word, she grabbed her purse and stormed out, slamming the front door behind her. Part of me immediately wondered if she was going over to Cam's, but the bigger part was just glad she was gone.

"What was all of that about?" Kori asked, turning to me.

"She wanted validation from me about Cam."

"They having issues?'

"Kori, I don't even think *they* know what's going on between them unless it involves condoms and handcuffs. And I'm only certain about them using one of those."

"Nyla, these flowers came for you."

"What?"

I turned to see Hailee, the front desk attendant, approaching me with a vase of pink carnations. She smiled as she set them on my desk.

"Someone must really be thinking about you today," she said, gently touching one of the flowers. "Either that or someone messed up."

"Hmph. Probably the latter. Thanks, Hailee."

I eyed the flowers as Hailee walked off. At least Kendrick remembered my favorite flower this time.

Not bothering to read the card, I went back to what I was doing. I had my interview for the manager position in a couple of hours and I was trying to make sure I was prepared. Zack had given me some of the questions I could expect to be asked and I wanted to have my answers on point.

"Cake in the break room!" I heard someone call out.

I loved me some cake, but I didn't need to risk getting frosting on my shirt or, as I managed to do one time, in my hair. It was already going to be enough of a task trying to keep my nerves from having me say something stupid.

I tried to chill out and remind myself that this was just something I was going for because it was there; it wasn't my life's dream. If it went well, great. If not, no skin off my potato.

When it was finally my time, I gave myself a quick check in my hand mirror and headed to the conference room where the interview was being held. Zack was already in there, along with a couple of the other higher-ups whose names I was racking my brain to remember.

"Nyla, come on in," Zack greeted with a smile, standing and running a hand through his floppy brown hair.

I returned his smile. "Hey, Zack."

"You remember Gilbert from headquarters and my direct superior, Carol?"

Thank god. "Yes, of course. Nice to see you two again."

"You too, Nyla," they chorused. Carol was smiling; Gilbert was already checking his watch.

"Please, have a seat, Nyla," Carol invited, motioning a manicured hand towards one of the empty seats across the conference table from her. "We were pleasantly surprised when we learned you were interested in moving up in the company."

"Oh, yes, well I figured now was a good time to make some moves," I stated, taking a seat and subtly rubbing my palms along my thighs under the table. "I feel established in my position and am ready for a new challenge."

"It's a *lot* more responsibility," Gilbert spoke up, turning his green eyes to me. "And while you have done well in your supervisory position, we want to be sure you're *really* aware of what you'd be taking on."

"Yes, I'm aware. Zack has been a great example these past few years. And I don't expect it to be a walk in the park but I'm sure I can handle whatever you throw at me."

Zack and Carol both looked pleased with my response, and Gilbert just pursed his lips and looked back at the tablet in front of him on the conference table.

The interview went on, with Carol and Zack asking me questions about leadership, future plans, what I'd do in certain scenarios, and just general things about the direction of the company. Gilbert occasionally chimed in with a question here and there, but for the most part he just let them handle the questioning while he inputted stuff on his tablet. For all I knew, he could've been updating a dating profile or doing a crossword puzzle, because he didn't seem totally engaged in the interview.

After about an hour, we finally wrapped things up.

"Well, Nyla, this has been very enlightening," Carol said, standing and tucking some of her gray bobbed hair behind her ear. "Thank you so much for your time."

"Thank *you*." I accepted her handshake, then Zack's, then – with decidedly less enthusiasm – Gilbert's. "I appreciate the consideration."

"We'll be in touch about next steps," Zack informed me, walking with me to the door. "You'll find out soon if you'll be moving forward with the next round of interviews."

There was going to be more of this? It's not like I was interviewing for the Pentagon.

"I'll look forward to hearing back either way," I made myself say with a smile.

He walked me over to the door, leaning down slightly when I was one foot across the threshold.

"Great job," he whispered.

I just grinned and nodded my thanks before heading back to my desk.

Well, that was done. At least I could breathe a little easier for the moment.

The rest of the workday went by as usual, and I figured I'd wait until I got home to call Kori. She'd already sent me several texts asking how things went.

I had to stop and get a few groceries on the way home, and when I got back to my apartment, I sighed when I looked at all of the stuff I had to carry inside. Purse, laptop bag, the dry cleaning that I'd been meaning to bring inside for days, and the groceries. The sensible thing would've been to just make two trips, but of course, I had to challenge myself to get it all in at one time. It was a good thing Zack, Carol or Gilbert weren't around to see this exceptional decision making.

I filled my arms and hands up with the bags and kicked the car door closed with my foot. Making sure I still had my keys in my hand already, I started to carefully head towards the building. But of course I dropped those keys four steps in.

"Ugh!"

I slowly stooped down, managing to grab my heart-shaped keychain with my fingertips before gingerly standing back up, my purse suddenly sliding off my shoulder, sending the other plastic grocery bags on that arm dropping to my wrist. The suddenness sent me bumping into my car, but I just cleared my throat and righted myself. My arms were already starting to hurt but I still (stupidly) refused to put any of the bags down.

Resuming my trek towards the building, I glanced up and suddenly hated that I lived on the second floor.

"Don't hit the curb...don't hit the curb..." I muttered to myself as I approached it. I tried to jerk my arms up to get the bags that had slid to my wrist back to my forearm. Doing that and still trying to walk wasn't the best idea.

I hit the curb.

My ass and all the bags hit the ground, and I yelped in pain. "Shit!"

"Nyla!"

He appeared in front of me so suddenly that I honestly thought I was dreaming. Did I hit my head?

"Cam? Wha-when did you get here? Where did you come from??"

"I just pulled up. Are you okay?" He reached down and gently removed the bags from my arms before helping me up. "Why are you trying to carry all of this in by yourself?"

"Who else is gonna do it? OW!"

"What? What's wrong??" He looked worried.

"My ankle..." I winced, nodding towards my right foot. "I must've twisted it..."

Without another word, he scooped me into his arms.

"Cam! What are you doing??"

"What does it look like I'm doing? I'm taking you to the hospital."

"I don't need to go the hospital. I'm sure once I ice it for a while and keep it wrapped, I'll be fine."

"I still think you should get it checked out. You never know."

"I'm sure nothing is broken."

"You don't know that."

"Cam..."

"Nyla, we need to be sure you're good."

I started to protest, then made the mistake of looking at him. He looked sincerely concerned, his adorable eyes looking right into mine. I became aware of the fact that his strong arms were holding me off the ground, the fingertips of his right hand gripping the underside of my upper thigh. His cologne, as usual, smelled spicy and delicious. And I resisted the urge to let my imagination morph this into some kind of post-marital situation instead of a post-accident one.

"Cam..." My small hands gripped him a little tighter. "I appreciate the concern, I really do. But believe me, I've twisted my ankle plenty over the years. This isn't anything new. Plus, I'd rather not go to the hospital and have to pay them for telling me what I already know."

That wary worried look was still in his eyes.

"Okay, look, if it's still really bad in a day or two, I'll go get it checked out," I promised him. "In the meantime, though, all I need you to do is just help me get my things inside."

"I'll get *you* inside and I'll carry all this stuff in myself."

"All right," I conceded, not having the energy to debate about it anymore. "At least hand me my purse and laptop bag, though."

Once I was settled in the living room and Cam had all of my groceries and things stashed, he went to work fixing an ice pack and finding a bandage to wrap my ankle. And he fussed whenever I even acted like I was going to try to get off the couch.

"Cam, this is so sweet of you," I commented as he adjusted the pillows under my foot. "Thank you for all of this. What brings you by, though? Were you looking for Jada?"

"No." He busied himself carefully wrapping the compression tape around my ankle. "Came to see you."

"Yeah?" I tried to get him to look at me but he wouldn't. "Not that I'm not glad to see you, but why?"

"We haven't been hanging out enough lately. And I know that's on me."

"I mean, I get it. You're in a relationship. I might not love it but I understand your girlfriend taking precedence over me."

"Yeah, well. It would be one thing if she deserved all that," he muttered. He reached for the ice pack. "But I'd much rather hang with you than deal with her, especially lately."

I wondered if Jada had told him about the latest squabble we had, and her threat to move out. Or if he knew about her night out with that other guy or her apparent doubts about their future. It made me wonder if Cam was having the same doubts.

"Cam," I sat up a little. "Talk to me. What's going on? I thought you were really into Jada but...I don't get that vibe from you. Are things okay?"

He sighed and dropped his hands. "Not really, no."

"What's going on?"

"I don't really want to talk about it, Nyla."

"Why? Why do you always shut down when it comes to that? You've talked about other girlfriends but when it comes to Jada, you've hardly shared anything with me. I don't need to know all of your business but I can't help but wonder why that is."

"I don't know...maybe Jada is different."

"Different...bad?"

"Just different. But yeah, some bad. I don't know how to explain it where it'll make any sense...being with her just doesn't feel the same as it did in the beginning and I'm still trying to figure out why."

"Have you talked to her about it?"

"We don't talk. I mean, she's tried to talk about us a few times and I admit I wasn't really trying to hear it."

"Why not? I mean, if you care about her, why not try to work things out, if you can?"

He looked at me for a moment, then suddenly turned away. Slapping his thighs, he stood up. "You have any alcohol in here?"

"Why are you changing the subject?"

"I just need a drink. And we can toast to your interview going well today."

"How do you know it went well?"

"Because if it didn't, you'd be in a way worse mood. And alcohol probably would've been in one of those bags you dropped. Then you'd be even *more* pissed about *that*."

"Don't be acting like you know me."

"Booze, Nyla."

"I don't have anything other than a couple of wine coolers."

"What are we, sixteen? I need some *real* alcohol. I'll go get some; you need anything else?"

"Food."

"Tacos?"

"Perfect."

"I'll be right back."

He left, and I shifted in my seat on the couch, wincing slightly at the pain in my ankle. I told myself that Cam showing up when he did was merely coincidence; didn't mean anything. Just like the fact that he seemed so troubled about his relationship with Jada, and that it looked like they were on their way to Splitsville. Even if they broke up that day, it didn't mean he'd discover any feelings for me. I'd be just as friend zoned as I already was.

Reminding myself of that helped distract from thinking about how good it felt to be in Cam's arms like I was earlier. He'd picked me up like it was nothing, which was a turn-on I was trying to ignore. His strength coupled with his immediate concern for me was threatening to send my feelings for him deeper into ridiculousness.

If only he loved me the way I loved him.

By the time Cam got back, I had updated Kori about my interview and (reluctantly) told her about Cam showing up right when I'd hurt myself again, and she of course took it as yet another sign that his feelings for me were more than friendly. Believe me, I'd love it if that were the case; I just didn't believe it was.

"All right, we've got tacos, alcohol, pain meds for your ankle in case you don't already have some..." Cam announced as he unloaded everything on the coffee table. "And I even swung by Starbucks for those cookies you love so much."

"Aww, Cam," I grinned. "You didn't have to do all that..."

"Shut up. I'm taking care of you tonight so you might as well just deal with it."

"Okay, fine. But don't think I don't notice that your alcohol-to-tacos ratio is a little off. I'm not really trying to get hammered. I *do* still have work tomorrow."

"Take the day off. You're a supervisor."

"That's not a justification for anything."

"Eat your tacos," he ordered, pushing three of them towards me. My stomach growled as I inhaled the scent of spicy beef and shrimp, my favorite combo. He loaded them up with pico de gallo and sour cream just like I liked 'em before moving on to his own.

"Thanks for this, Cam," I said after a few moments of us stuffing our faces. "I'm glad you decided to come by today."

"Me, too."

"Maybe if you start drinking, you'll be willing to talk about what's going on with you and Jada."

"You're thinking about that more than I am. I'm just trying to hang with *you* right now."

"All right, fine." I didn't know why I was pressing so hard to talk about it, anyway. It wasn't like I was gung-ho about them staying together. It should've made me happy that he seemed like he was as done with Jada as she seemed to be with him.

Well, I was done worrying about it. My obligatory concern over their relationship quota had been met and now I was just going to enjoy having Cam to myself for once. And it felt good, us talking and laughing and clowning like we did before Jada came into the picture.

We polished off the rest of the tacos before moving on to the booze, downing glass after glass of Hennessey and wine. At some point I'd thrown caution to the wind and stopped counting how many glasses I had. Looked like I just *might* be taking off work the next day.

"Hey," he barked, burping into his fist before looking at me. "What's the deal with you and that Kevin busta?"

"Who?"

"The big dude you were slobbin' down in the middle of the living room."

"Oh, Kendrick. Nothin'." I downed the last of my wine.

"Y'all ain't together?"

"No. We just had sex. Didn't mean anything." I must've really been drunk because that's not something I would've disclosed to him sober.

"Y-you what??" His head snapped towards me. "You *fucked* him??"

"So what? Don't you *fuck* Jada??" I countered, returning his glare. "At least you didn't hear me doing it like I heard y'all."

"I can't believe you did that," he muttered. He snatched one of my cookies from the bag.

"Hey! Those are *my* cookies!"

"You don't seem to mind sharing your *cookies* any other time." He looked right at me as he took a huge bite out of the chocolate chip cookie. "So you shouldn't care now."

"Ugh, you get on my *nerves*!" I exclaimed, stupidly kicking him with the foot of my hurt ankle. "Ouch!"

"See there? Went and hurt yourself again."

"Maybe if you weren't acting so stupid..."

"Maybe if you weren't out fuckin' other dudes..."

"Can you stop saying that? And I have desires like everybody else. I don't see you keepin' it in *your* pants. If I wanna sleep with Kendrick or anybody else, I'll *do* it!"

"Don't play with me, Nyla! Don't even play with me!"

"Don't play with *me*!"

"Take back what you just said!" He dropped the rest of the cookie onto the table and grabbed my arms. "Take it back!"

"Why should I? I meant it! Hell, *you* don't want me...I'd think you'd be happy for me when there's someone who does, since we're supposed to be *friends* and all!"

A strange look flashed across his face. "Who said I didn't want you?"

His question froze me. "W-what?"

"I'm asking where you're getting your information from. 'Cause *I* certainly never told you that."

He's drunk. That's the only reason he's saying this.

"Whatever, Cam," I dismissed, even though his words had me tingling in dangerous places. "You've clearly had too much Hennessey. Go get some water."

"I don't need any water."

"You're drunk. We're both drunk."

"I know exactly what I'm sayin'," he insisted, his grip on my arms tightening a little. "And doing."

Before I could blink, his lips were on mine. Then his tongue was in my mouth.

It took several seconds before it registered in my brain that Cam was kissing me. Like I had fantasized about so many times, *he was kissing me*. I moaned because I couldn't help it, my lips automatically responding to his. He grunted deeply as he pushed himself up my body further, his hand coming up to grab the side of my face and neck.

"Shit," I whimpered as he slid his tongue up the other side of my neck to my ear, tracing around the edge before sucking on my earlobe. I didn't even know I liked that but it was surely turning on the floodgates down below. I writhed beneath him, wishing he would get all the way on top of me. My hands gripped the back of his shirt, hating that it was keeping me from touching his skin. I wanted to touch his everything.

"*Fuck*, Nyla," he growled, overtaking my mouth again. His hand grabbed my breast and my back arched so hard I'm surprised I didn't hurt myself. "I knew it..."

"Cam..." My hands palmed his face. "Oh my god..."

We continued to make out in our drunken stupor, with Cam repeatedly whispering "I knew it." I was too out of it to ask what he meant by that; I just wanted to enjoy the moment.

He climbed on top of me, being mindful of my hurt ankle, and I almost came right then when I felt his hardness pressing against me. The leg with my hurt ankle lifted around his waist so he could get even closer. When he began that delicious slow grind, all of the fantasies about him and I making love came roaring back. And in those fantasies, we were in love...and sober. That wasn't the case here, on either count.

Well, *I* was in love. He just didn't know it.

"Cam," I breathed, reluctantly pushing against his chest. "We should...we should stop."

"Huh? What's wrong?" He leaned up to look at me. I could see glassiness in his eyes. This whole scene was just an impulsive drunken indulgence, and as much as I wanted it, I didn't want it like this. If we took it there, I wanted us both fully in our right minds so it couldn't be blamed on anything other than our fire for each other.

"You're drunk," I reminded him, gently placing a hand over his mouth when he tried to kiss me again. It took *every* bit of willpower I had. "Hell, *I'm* drunk. This probably isn't something we should be doing right now."

"You don't want to?" He bit his lower lip as he pressed his rock-hardness against me again, and my eyes fluttered closed briefly. He had no idea...I wanted Cam inside of me more than all the tacos and cookies in the city. But he probably wouldn't even remember this in the morning while I already knew it was going to cloud my mind indefinitely.

"You're drunk, Cam," I reminded rather than confirming my desire. "Drunk sex isn't...we shouldn't."

He peered down at me, his chest still heaving. I could smell the alcohol on his breath and feel his pulsing erection through his pants. I thought he was going to try to convince me to change my mind or insist he wasn't that drunk, but he just suddenly pushed himself off of me. He sat at the other end of the couch, running his hands down his face. Part of me knew I'd done the right thing by shutting things down, but the other part hated that it was necessary.

I tried to ignore how ridiculously horny I still was as I dug my fists into the couch, pushing myself upright. I could still feel where his hands touched my body, namely my breasts. They ached to be touched by him again already, and I had to literally bite my lips to keep myself from taking back everything I just said and pulling him back on top of me.

"Sorry," Cam muttered, his eyes on the floor.

"No, it's...it's fine," I quickly assured, reaching a hand towards him before letting it fall back into my lap. "No need to apologize."

Several awkward moments passed before he finally turned and looked at me. His eyes were intense and unwavering as they looked right into mine, and I wondered what was going through his mind. If he hated that I stopped him or if he was regretting it already. And I surely wasn't about to ask.

Finally, we both spoke up at once.

"Nyla, maybe we should-"

"Cam, do you-"

The door opened, causing us both to jump. I'd totally forgotten about Jada.

She looked mildly surprised to see Cam there, and her eyes roamed over the mess from our dinner on the coffee table and the empty alcohol bottles. Her eyes took on an almost accusatory slant, as if she just knew she had walked in on something.

Honey, if only you'd walked in three minutes ago.

"I didn't know you were gonna be over here," Jada said to Cam, not even acknowledging me. "But I guess I shouldn't be surprised."

"It's not like I know where you're coming from right now, either," Cam quickly countered, returning her slight frown. "Just like you don't tell me your every move, I don't tell you mine."

"I left you a message."

"I know."

"So we're just ignoring each other's messages now?"

"Doesn't feel good, huh? Because there have been more than a few times when you ignored mine."

"I didn't *ignore* anything; I just didn't respond right away."

"Okay, well I'll answer yours tomorrow, then."

"Cam." She put her hand on her hip and I just sat there in the middle of this tense exchange, tangling my fingers and trying to keep my eyes on the houseplant across the room.

"Jada." He returned her pointed look.

"Let's...can we go to my room?"

"I don't need to go to your room. I'm good where I am."

Jada's eyes flitted to me, as if I was making him say this. She took a step towards Cam. "I really think we need to talk. Please?"

Cam glanced at me, but I only slightly hunched my shoulders, indicating I had nothing to do with this. Finally, he shot off the couch, wobbling only slightly.

"Come to think of it, you're right," he said to Jada. "We *do* need to have a talk. Let's go." He looked at me. "Don't move, Nyla; I'll be back. It's still me and you tonight."

They went to Jada's room and closed the door, and I just continued to sit there, wondering if they were about to finally break up or if Cam was going to pick up with her where he'd left off with me.

"If I hear bed springs, it's a *wrap*," I muttered.

Chapter 10

"So did he dump her?"

"For the tenth time, Kori, I didn't come over here to talk about this."

"I don't see why not. You had to know I was gonna ask when you told me Jada caught you and Cam getting it in on the couch."

"That is not what happened."

"Kissing and grinding...same thing."

"It's not, Kori."

"I don't know why you're not happy about this, Nyla. The man you've wanted since you met him finally made his move. You should be bouncing off the walls."

"Kori, come on..." I sighed as I placed the gourmet chocolates into the gift bags I was helping her assemble for her grand opening at Sleek. "He was drunk. We were *both* drunk. The kiss doesn't count; he probably doesn't even know he did it."

"So I take it you two haven't talked about it, then."

"About that, no. But he *did* tell me that Jada wanted them to take things to the next level and threw a whole fit when he hesitated to agree to it."

"Oooh!" Kori exclaimed, dropping the empty bag she just picked up. "So they broke up? He dumped her for you?"

"I didn't say all that. I don't even *know* if they broke up."

"I bet he did. And I bet I know why."

"I'm sure you'll enlighten me, regardless, so..."

"Because he wants you. He finally realized he wants to be with *you*."

"Are *you* drunk right now?"

"Nyla, come on," Kori threw up her hands, sitting back in her chair. "We've both been drunk before. You know as well as I do that alcohol only emboldens you, it doesn't inhibit you. Cam probably only used alcohol to finally push him towards what he's been wanting to do for months."

Maybe what she said made some sense. But I knew better than to get my hopes up. Even though I'd been daydreaming about Cam's kiss more than a few times a day since it happened, I wasn't trying to be foolish. Cam and I had talked and hung out several times since that day and he hadn't even mentioned it. For all I knew, he didn't even remember the damn kiss.

The only thing I knew for sure was that I couldn't sit around waiting for Cam to start seeing me in a more romantic light. And I admit that I didn't have the nerve to just come out and ask him if he remembered kissing me; I started to a couple of times since but always lost my nerve (as usual). He was acting like it never happened and it was easier to just follow his lead.

But whether Cam remembered the kiss or not, I certainly did. All the alcohol we had that night didn't keep me from recalling every ping that shot through my body when he put his lips and hands on me, and laid his body on top of mine. Every night I wished he would appear in my bedroom for a repeat performance. As if I hadn't already been fantasizing about this man enough.

Jada hadn't been home much since her and Cam's (latest) big argument, which I wasn't mad at. When she *was* there, she practically ignored me. I didn't know where she was in her moving-out process, and for the time being, I wasn't pushing her on it. It wasn't like I didn't need her rent money. As long as she didn't try to start any more trouble with me, I'd be patient.

I hated this feeling of being in limbo, though; not knowing what was going on with Cam and Jada meant that I didn't know what could happen with me and Cam. That is, if Cam was even really interested in me like that at all, which was still the big question. I had to do something to see if things had changed any.

My opportunity came when I heard Jada on the phone in the kitchen one Sunday morning, telling someone that Cam would be coming over at around six so they could 'work some things out.' Didn't know what *that* meant, but Kori's advice about getting Cam to see me differently rang through my head.

So by the time Cam showed up a few hours later, I was dolled up in some freshly-made cutoff shorts, three-inch ankle booties, and a leather bomber jacket over my boobs-enhancing camisole. (What the good lord didn't give me in height, he gave me in ta-tas. I had a *really* nice set of girls, if I do say so myself).

I'd carefully styled my short hair and applied noticeable but still not overdone makeup, enhancing my light eyes with liner and mascara and busting out the good matte lipstick. Large hoop earrings and a long silver chain completed the look. I stepped back in my full-length mirror and couldn't help but grin; I looked damn sexy. Felt even sexier. I couldn't even remember the last time I'd done myself up like this, but maybe I needed to do it more often.

I stayed in my room until I heard the knock on the front door, and then Cam and Jada talking in the living room. Before they could retreat to her bedroom or leave, I hurried to emerge, my purse slung over my shoulder.

Both Cam and Jada's jaws dropped when they saw me, and I didn't try to hide my smile at that. I rather loved it.

"Damn!" Cam exclaimed. "Where are *you* going??"

"Oh, hey Cam," I replied coolly. "I didn't know you were coming over here."

"Yeah, I just came to...*damn*!"

Jada glared at him. "You don't have to act like you've never seen short shorts before. I wear those all the time."

"Uh-huh." Cam's eyes were still on me, taking everything in. And I might not have been the best at reading men, but I knew lust-filled appreciation when I saw it. My whole body warmed at the sight.

"Nyla, I've never seen you look like this before," Jada observed, easing in front of Cam as if that would stop him from ogling me. "You have a hot date or something?"

"Or something," I winked, grinning. Cam was looking at me, chest heaving slightly, and I wondered what he would do if Jada wasn't standing there. His eyes dipped to the chain nestled in my cleavage, then back to my face. His eyes seemed even darker. "I'm just gonna find my keys and then I'll be out of your way."

"Where, um..." He cleared his throat. "You hanging out with Kori?"

"Nope."

"Oh. That big dude?"

"You know his name, Cam. But no, I'm not seeing Kendrick."

"It's just that I've never seen you look so..." He cleared his throat again and Jada turned to look at him, as interested in the following adjective as I was. I arched an expectant brow.

"So...?" I urged when he still didn't speak after a couple of moments.

"Hot," Cam finally finished. "You look damn hot, Nyla."

Jada looked at him for a moment, then turned her eyes to me thoughtfully. I pretended not to notice.

"Well, thank you, Cam." I winked at him, then raked some hair from my forehead with my freshly-painted red nails. "Jada, have you seen my keys laying around?"

"You usually keep them in the little bowl by the door."

"Shoot." I tapped my foot and darted my eyes around the room with a hand on my hip. Moving over to the couch, I turned my back to them and leaned over to slide my hand between the couch cushions. My ass was in the air as I rested a knee on the couch to find the keys I'd snuck in and hid there earlier, and I had to resist the urge to glance back and see Cam's reaction. Part of me felt I was going a tad overboard with this, but the other part was thoroughly enjoying it.

"Found 'em," I announced, standing with my keys in hand. "They must have fallen out of my pocket or something. Anyway, I'll leave you two alone..."

"I, uh..." Cam spoke up before I reached the door. "I'm not sure you should be going out by yourself...like that. I can come with you-"

"Uh, *what*?" Jada snapped, frowning at him. "You came over here so we could talk, Cam; you remember that?"

"Yeah, I'm fine, Cam; stay here with your girl." I opened the door, noting how his expression shifted at my comment. "I'll talk to you later. Y'all have fun."

"Let me know when you get wherever you're going," Cam quickly ordered.

"I'm fine, Cam," I said again, my voice almost taking a singsong tone. I closed the door to Cam's intrigued yet confused expression, and Jada's annoyed one.

That went better than I thought it would.

Cam looked like he wanted to jump me, and I had to wonder if he would have if we'd been alone. So I was pretty sure he was attracted to me physically. The only question was how deep it ran. But I could take solace in knowing that the image of me looking like this would likely stay stuck in Cam's mind beyond tonight. Which hopefully would mean he'd stop just seeing me as the platonic friend he felt responsible for and start looking at me like a woman he wanted to explore a relationship with.

Once in my car, I snapped a couple of driver's seat selfies because I was looking too cute not to, and looked at the full-length shots I'd taken earlier in my room. I certainly didn't hate the look, even though it wasn't something I could see myself doing every day. But maybe it wouldn't hurt to spruce myself up more often, just because it felt so good to do so. I actually felt, as Cam said, damn hot.

Now if only I had somewhere to go.

I actually had no plans to go anywhere; this was all about letting Cam see me in a new light and that was it. Maybe I should've made a date or set something in place, but I admittedly didn't think that far ahead.

Before I could start to feel silly about that, my phone rang. When I saw Kendrick's name, I perked up a tiny bit. Maybe this look would get a little more stretch out of it, after all.

"Hey, Nyla," he greeted when I answered. "What you up to?"

"Nothing much. What's up, Kendrick?"

"I was trying to see if you wanted to link up tonight. I miss you."

"Oh...what is it you wanna do?"

"You can just come over and hang. I'll fix us something to eat and we can just cuddle up the rest of the night; watch a movie or whatever."

In other words, the same thing we usually do. Kendrick didn't even try to actually take me on dates anymore; there'd only been one time since we'd semi-reconnected that he offered to take me out. Any other time it was on some *come over and chill* stuff. Yeah, he cooked for me and I loved his cooking. And I loved a night in just fine. But for all his claims of wanting me back so much, he sure wasn't putting forth a lot of effort. Would this be all we did if we got back together? Dinner and movies and quiet, sweaty sex in his apartment?

Just like that, I realized I wasn't interested in finding out.

Kendrick wasn't the man I wanted. I only considered getting back with him at all because I felt I'd never get Cam. But I didn't need or want to settle. That wouldn't be fair to either one of us.

"Kendrick, umm..." I scratched the back of my neck. "I'm sorry but it's probably best that we stop this."

"Stop what?"

"Seeing each other."

There was a pause. "Why? What did I do?"

"You didn't do anything, Kendrick. It's just that I'm realizing that us getting back together isn't what I really want. And I don't want to waste your time."

"Just like that? You're *just* realizing that now?"

"Honestly, yes; I've been going back and forth about it for weeks but now I'm sure. I'd just rather not go there with you again."

"Wow, Nyla," he scoffed, sucking his teeth. "So what is it we've been doing, huh? You'll come over and eat my food and kiss on me and get in my bed, but you *don't wanna go there with me again.* That's *real* convenient."

"What? Kendrick, let's not do this, okay? This doesn't have to get ugly. It's not like I said I didn't want anything else to do with you; I just don't want a romantic relationship."

"Well, I do. But I guess that doesn't matter, huh?"

My head fell back against the headrest. "Kendrick..."

"I don't know why you're acting like you're tired of *me*. You're not the one that just got tossed in the gutter like some chewing gum you done sucked all the flavor out of."

"I'm not doing this with you. If you can't accept this like an adult, then we need to just go ahead and end this conversation."

"Yeah, whatever."

"Hopefully we can talk sometime when you're not in your feelings and are willing to be more rational. In any case, thank you for the flowers."

"What? I didn't send you no flowers. You must have me confused with one of the *other* brothas you're messing with. Hopefully you're jerking them around like you did me." He hung up.

Shaking my head, I dropped my phone onto the passenger's seat. I guess I shouldn't have expected him to take that well. When I broke up with Kendrick the first time, he straight cussed me out, so this wasn't as bad.

His words just occurring to me, I grabbed my purse and dug for the card that came with the flowers that were delivered to me at work a few days earlier. I'd never even bothered to read it, assuming they'd been from Kendrick. But I was mistaken.

I hope these make you smile; I like being the one to do that.

And don't stress about the interview. Just go kill it.

Love you,
Cam

My hand pressed to my chest as I released a small breath. It didn't even occur to me that Cam could've been the one to send me those and knowing that he did warmed me to the bone. I started to call and thank him, but remembered he was probably still with Jada *working things out*.

Figuring I might as well not totally waste my outfit, I headed to Costco to fill up on free samples.

By the time I got back to the apartment, Cam was gone and Jada was in her room surrounded by suitcases.

"Oh…" I paused at her bedroom door.

"Yep," Jada confirmed my unasked question as she yanked some clothes from her closet. "I'm leaving."

Pursing my lips, I looked at the mess in her room as I shifted my weight. "I take it you and Cam couldn't work things out."

"Nope." She glanced at me but kept stuffing clothes into bags. "He doesn't seem to know what he wants and I'm not trying to wait forever. So...that's that."

I felt like I should say that I was sorry to hear that, but that would be a lie that she probably wouldn't believe, anyway. It was hard enough fighting the smile that was tugging at my mouth.

"Where are you gonna go?" I asked instead.

"Back to my ex," she muttered, tucking some hair behind her ear. "I called him and was freaking out; he managed to calm me down and told me to just get my stuff and come back to him. So that's where I'm going. At least *he's* sure of what he wants."

"Wow..." All I was hearing was that Cam was officially a free man. He had sent me a couple of texts since I left but I hadn't responded yet; now I was wishing Jada would hurry up and leave so I could call him back.

"I'm sorry that I didn't give you more notice than this," Jada continued. "You already have my rent for the month so hopefully that'll be good enough. I just don't want to be here where I can keep running into Cam. 'Cause he'll surely be back over here to see you."

The way she grumbled that last part made me wonder if I'd been the topic of discussion at all after I left. Jada never did like it when Cam paid me more than passing attention. And he hadn't been able to take his eyes off me earlier. Jada surely noticed that and called him on it when they were alone.

"I'll manage," I told her, hoping that was true. With her gone, I'd really have to tighten my purse strings. But I'd be okay for a while. "You...you take care of yourself, Jada."

"That's exactly what I'm doing." She snapped the last suitcase closed and put it with the others at the foot of the bed. She paused to look at me, her brown eyes roaming. "Enjoy yourself?"

"Oh...yeah, I had a nice time." The nice lady in frozen foods at Costco let me have all the pigs in a blanket I wanted (I might've given her the impression that I'd been stood up so I wouldn't be the crazy woman who got dressed up just to go to a grocery store). And one station had mini crab cakes so...score. "It was quite the interesting evening. But now I need to get out of these shoes. You're leaving tonight?"

"Yep, tonight. I'll leave the key."

"Okay, then." Feeling like there wasn't anything else to say, I eased away from her doorway and went to my room, closing the door behind me.

Cam and Jada were over.

I was both giddy and nervous about that. Giddy because there was nothing standing between something happening between me and Cam; nervous because I still wasn't sure if Cam really *wanted* anything to happen between us. I wanted to call him but didn't want to do it with Jada still there.

By the time she finally left, though, I was in my pajamas, fighting sleep as I watched HGTV. She barely said goodbye as she hauled her bags out the door. And I didn't even hear my phone when Cam called.

Chapter 11

"Such an idiot," I muttered as I loaded my Home Depot purchases into my backseat. Shopping for anything that wasn't a necessity was the last thing I needed to be doing, but since Jada moved out, I'd become obsessed with improving the apartment. I got a new coffee table from someone off Facebook Marketplace, new curtains for my bedroom, a better showerhead. Redoing the kitchen counters was going to be my project for the coming weekend, hence the trip to Home Depot. The landlord was cool with it. I just ignored the little voice in my head reminding me of the bills on my counter waiting to be paid.

Throwing myself into home improvement was also another way to keep my mind off the fact that Cam and I still hadn't talked. I called him the day after Jada moved out, but it went to voicemail. After a couple more calls, I figured I'd just let him call me; maybe he was busy with work or smarting over ending things with Jada more than expected. Either way, I wasn't going to chase him.

So I just focused on doing my own thing, and helping Kori with her boutique. Sleek's grand opening had gone wonderfully, and Kori had been rather busy her first couple of weeks of business. I went by to help her out when I could, or to keep her company while she got things closed up in the evenings. She was exhausted but happier; much happier than she'd been at BryCom. And seeing her do her own thing was so inspiring; she hadn't been satisfied with how her life was going and she did something about it. I needed to take a page from her book.

If only I knew exactly what to do.

I still hadn't heard back about the promotion at work, which I still wasn't even sure I really wanted. As inspired as I was by Kori, I didn't think being an entrepreneur was my calling. I wanted to just go to work during certain times and be off the rest of the time. But I was just realizing that I never took the time to decide what I'd love to do; I just got jobs that paid the bills.

Cam was still on my mind and in my heart, but the uncertainty about the future of our friendship was starting to creep back in. I was back to thinking that he was never going to see me as anything other than a friend, despite our drunken kiss and his momentary lust at seeing me dolled up. And I had to decide if I could be okay with that.

There was a knock on my door and I cursed myself for immediately hoping it was Cam. If we were going to remain friends, I'd definitely have to learn how to wean myself off of these feelings for him.

When I checked the peephole, I was a little surprised to see a woman standing there.

"Hey Nyla," Jenny, my neighbor, greeted once I opened the door. "Sorry to bother you..."

"No bother. What's up?"

"I was wondering if you had any flour. I'm baking some muffins and accidentally dropped mine on the floor. Tripped over my own foot. I'm such a klutz sometimes."

"Believe me, I can relate. Yeah, I think I have some flour; come on in while I take a look."

"Great, thanks."

She stepped inside and closed the door behind her while I went to check my flour supply. I had about half a bag left, and when I went back to the living room, Jenny was curiously glancing around.

"Here you go," I held the bag out to her. "You can just take the rest, if you need it. Hope it's enough."

"Oh this is great, thanks *so* much, Nyla," Jenny gushed, grabbing the bag and grinning gratefully. "I was so hoping I wouldn't have to go to the store. But when I get groceries this weekend, I'll definitely replace this for you."

"That's fine. It's no problem, really."

"Hey, I love what you've done in here," she commented, tucking some curly hair behind her ear as she turned her eyes back to my living room.

"Oh, thanks."

"It's so cute and homey. I have zero eye for decorating; you should see my place. Bare bones."

"I appreciate it, though I'm certainly no expert, either. I've always loved this kind of stuff; even used to redesign my Barbie dream houses back in the day. That and years of watching HGTV have seeped in, I guess."

"Ugh, I tried watching a couple of those shows and could never get into it. It's just not my thing. Hey, do you think you'd be willing to come look at my place sometime and suggest ways I can spruce things up? My dad actually gave me some money to get some furniture and decorating stuff but, again, I suck at it and have no clue what to get."

I chuckled. "You can't be that bad."

"Nyla, I'm so serious. I'm good at baking, which is why I just started my own little side business. But home design? Nada. *Please*, help me out; I'm tired of my place looking like a 'before' picture. I'll pay you."

My ears perked up.

"I guess I can come over and see what you're working with," I replied with admittedly more enthusiasm. "Just let me know when a good time for me would be to come take a look."

"Great!" She actually jumped up and down a little bit, clutching the bag of flour with both hands and grinning like she'd just won a prize. I just hoped she didn't drop that flour all over my new rug. "I'll get with you in a couple of days, okay?"

"That'll work. And congrats on the new business."

"Thanks!"

She scurried out, happy as could be, and I found myself actually looking forward to this little project. I'd helped Kori decorate her place, and Sleek. And Cam's house was nothing but sports memorabilia and black before I got my hands on it.

Remembering that made me think of how much fun he and I had together during that process. We spent entire weekends together, shopping for things, painting, and just hanging out. That was when our friendship really deepened and we hit 'best friend' status. We learned so much about each other, sitting around his place eating takeout or taking a mini road trip for the sofa he didn't think he needed, but loved once it was in his living room.

I felt myself starting to ache, missing that.

My phone rang, and I actually gasped when I saw it was Cam. Maybe if I thought real hard about a check arriving in my mailbox, that would actually happen, too.

"You got some time for me to come over?" he wasted no time asking.

"Yeah...you okay?"

"Not really," he grumbled. "I'll be there in a few minutes."

My frown was curious as I hung up the phone and automatically rushed to the bathroom to check my face and hair. He sounded weird; like something was really bothering him. I wondered if he wanted to vent about Jada or if something else was on his mind.

I didn't have to wait long to find out because he was knocking on my door in the next couple of minutes. He must have called me from the parking lot.

"What's up?" I asked as he stormed into my apartment.

"Did you know Jada moved in with her ex?"

"Yeah."

His head snapped to me. "What??"

"Yeah, I knew. She told me when she was leaving."

"And you didn't tell me??"

"Why would I think to tell you that, Cam? One, you two had broken up so I figured you wouldn't care, and two, I assumed that was something she would have told you herself."

"Well, you were wrong."

"So...what, you're mad at *me* now?"

"You should've told me that, Nyla," he barked, taking off his jacket and throwing it onto the couch. "But I guess I shouldn't be surprised, since you've barely been there for me during this entire thing."

My jaw dropped. "Excuse me??"

"Don't try to act like you don't know what I'm talking about, Nyla! I'm supposed to be your boy yet when I get dumped, by *your* roommate, I hardly hear from you!"

"Are you serious with this? I *called* you, Cam! More than once! *You're* the one who went all scarce! I figured you needed some time to yourself so I let you have it!"

"Oh, *you let me have it*," he mocked, stopping his pacing to glare at me. "Thanks a lot. You should've tried harder, Nyla."

"What was I supposed to do, Cam? Show up at your house and force you to feel better? Hell, I couldn't have known you were all that distraught, anyway, since you never let on that she meant that much to you. Are you trying to say you were in love with her?"

He paused, then looked away. "No."

"That's what I thought. Especially since *you're* the reason you two broke up, seeing as how you weren't ready to move forward like she was. So why the hell are you even this upset?"

"How are you not getting this?" He came and stood right in front of me, and I told myself to ignore how delicious he smelled. "Regardless, you should've been doing everything *possible* to be there for me but I honestly wonder if you even gave a damn. You never seemed to be that supportive of me and Jada being together, anyway."

"Maybe I wasn't," I huffed, folding my arms and returning his scowl. "Maybe I was pissed that you got with Jada in the first place!"

"Why? Why would you say some shit like that??"

"Because I wanted you to be with *me*, Cam!"

It just came out, but I didn't try to take it back. I wasn't going to get a better opening than that and I needed to *finally* get it off my chest.

Cam was the picture of shock, stepping back with his jaw practically to his chest.

"Are you for real?" he finally asked after several pensive moments.

"I wouldn't lie about that, Cam." My face was burning and my chest was heaving, but now it was as much from nervousness about what he was going to say than the anger that was causing it before.

"Shit." He ran a hand over the top of his head and down his face, backing up a couple more steps. "Why...how long have you..." He sat on the arm of the couch and finally looked up at me. "Why didn't you say anything before now?"

I released a sarcastic chuckle as I dropped my hands. "For what? It's not like you felt the same way."

He opened his mouth to say something, but nothing came out.

"You made it perfectly clear that friends is all we'll ever be, Cam," I continued, on a roll. "You don't want anything to change; remember saying that? So I wasn't in a huge hurry to make a fool of myself by telling you that I've been in love with you since the day we met. Or that you getting with my roommate was like a kick in the teeth, and every time I saw you kiss her or heard you *fucking* her in the next room was like heart-frying torture. Did you really wanna hear that??"

"Nyla, I..."

"There was no point and I knew it, so I kept it to myself." I went and stood right in front of him, getting in his face so he had to look at me. "And since we're *sharing* and everything, you might as well also know that I've been wondering if our friendship is something that needs to continue."

His eyes widened. "What?"

"I'm not sure this is healthy for me, Cam." My voice had lowered almost to a whisper, and I felt the tears stinging my eyes. Just as they always did when I thought about Cam no longer being in my life. "The whole thing about being in love with my best friend would be cute if this was a romance novel or movie and I was sure that we'd end up together in the end, but I don't know that. You don't see me as anything other than your little baby-faced friend that you might love-"

"I *do* love," he urgently interrupted, grabbing my hands. "Nyla, you *know* I love you."

"But not like I love *you*, and we both know it," I retorted. The tears were streaming down my face and I didn't try to stop them. Cam looked at me, pained; he always hated to see me cry. "And I just...I don't know if I can keep doing this. Watching you with other women...if it's not Jada, it'll be somebody else. And it honestly just hurts too much."

"Nyla...I had no idea, I swear." He palmed both sides of my face, wiping my tears with his thumbs. "You know I'd never knowingly do anything to hurt you. Please tell me you know that."

"I know, Cam." I sniffed. "I'm not trying to say you did anything wrong. I can't expect you to read my mind. But..." I stepped back, easing away from his touch. "This is just what it is."

"What about Kendrick?"

"I never got back with Kendrick. I only considered it to try to get over you but decided it wasn't what I really wanted. And I wasn't about to waste his time like that."

"Can we please talk about this?" He stood, following me as I inched away. "'Cause you're trying to...you're trying to end our friendship and I'm not okay with that. Not at all, Nyla."

"Well, I don't know what you expect me to do, Cam." I threw up my hands, looking up at him with my watery eyes. "Just get over it? Hope that it fades over time? We've been friends for over a year and it hasn't faded at all; if anything, it's only intensified. So you tell me how we can possibly keep this going now that you know the truth?"

"Nothing has to end. How 'bout if I just...what if I-"

"Cam, I can't..."

"Nyla!"

"Do you remember kissing me?" I glared right into his eyes, which were looking into mine pleadingly. He blinked at my question.

"What?"

"Do you remember touching me, laying your body on mine? *I* do, and it was amazing. And I haven't been able to stop thinking about it since it happened. But I bet you have no idea what I'm talking about, do you?"

He hesitated, and I scoffed, shaking my head. I'd been holding out some small shred of hope that he'd remember that night and even that he'd enjoyed it as much as I had. But just as I figured, it had meant nothing to him. Nothing at all.

I turned away from him.

"Cam, I need you to leave," I stated, wiping my eyes with both hands. "I can't do this with you anymore."

I felt his hands on my shoulders. "Nyla, please..."

Shaking my head, I moved away. "Please don't. You have no idea how much I *don't* wanna be saying this right now and it's taking every ounce of strength I have to do it. So please just...give me this, okay?"

He didn't move for what seemed like forever. And as long as he stood behind me, I kept my back to him, crying quietly.

Finally, he left. And as soon as I heard the door close, the tears turned back up to full blast.

"What did I just do??" I exclaimed, whirling around towards the door as if I hoped to see him still standing there. "Oh my god!"

Did I really just end my friendship with Cam? Was that the last time I'd see him? The thought made my chest hurt, and I groped for the nearest wall because it really felt like I was about to fall over.

I eyed my phone, already wanting to call him. Or hoping he'd call me. And I don't know how many minutes I stood there staring at it. When it stayed silent, I clamped a hand over my mouth as a new wave of tears blurred my vision.

"Stop it," I finally whispered to myself, trying to calm down. "You just did what you needed to do."

Knowing that didn't stop the pain, though. And I knew I wouldn't be getting over it any time soon. So I allowed myself ten good minutes to cry, and I used every one of them.

Chapter 12

Cam blew up my phone with voicemails and texts for a good week after I confessed my feelings to him and ended the friendship. I listened to every voicemail and read every text but didn't respond. I *so* wanted to, but I knew doing that would just prolong my getting past this.

Then the calls and texts started to taper off, and I wasn't sure what hurt worse; the fact that I had to end my friendship with Cam or the fact that he seemed to start to be okay with it.

"Nyla, sweetie...you haven't acknowledged any of his messages," Kori gently reminded after my fifteenth time whining about this, handing me a beer. "How long did you expect him to keep reaching out to you and getting nothing?"

"I don't know," I admitted, sniffling as I stared at the bottle in my hand. "Maybe it's unreasonable but...I just wanted him to keep trying. It's like he's giving up on me for good."

"Like you gave up on him?"

I glared at her. "Whose side are you on?"

"Absolutely yours. But that doesn't mean that I'm not gonna be real with you. Nyla, girl, I get you wanting to protect yourself. But you didn't even give the man a chance. You sprung your feelings on him in the middle of an argument and when he was still shellshocked, you pushed him out the door. And now that you both have had a few days to process things, you're *still* not talking to him."

She had a point; I acknowledged that. I suppose I didn't consider how I *actually* handled this:

Bam, I'm in love with you.

Bam, we kissed a little while ago, do you remember? Answer quick. Oop, not quick enough.

Bam, we need to end this friendship. Right now. Oh, and get out.

"Damn it," I muttered, clunking the beer on the coffee table and dropping my head into my hands. I didn't even care about using a coaster, I was so distraught. "How did I manage to mess this up?"

"Raw adrenaline and emotion. The way you described it, Cam set that snowball of truth in motion when he came in here fussing about Jada. You didn't have time to plan out how you were gonna break things to him."

"True. This was certainly unplanned."

"It's understandable. But I just hope you don't leave Cam hanging like that. Remember, his *only* sin is not reciprocating your romantic feelings, which isn't something you can force. As far as friendship goes, he did nothing wrong, yet you're punishing him like he did."

"That's not what I'm trying to do, Kori, I swear," I whined, falling to my side dramatically on the couch. "I clearly wasn't looking at any of this from his side; I was only thinking about what I needed to do for myself. It felt like the right thing at the time but the more I think about it now, the worse I feel. Cam didn't deserve that."

"Then fix it, girl. Even if at the end of it you think that you still need to separate yourself from Cam, at least give the man a chance to say his piece. Give the brother *that* much."

She was right. I buried my face in a pillow and groaned.

"All right; I'll call him."

So I did. And this time I tried to have at least some idea of what I was going to say, since freestyling this kind of thing clearly wasn't my bag. There was even a little tiny part of me that hoped Cam would have realized he was in love with me too, and we could meet up and kiss and make love and get married and live blissfully ever after.

But Cam wasn't as receptive to my call as I expected.

"Oh, so you're talking to me now, huh?" This was how he answered the phone.

"Uhh..." That stumped me a little but I tried to get it together. "Cam, I know you're probably upset about how things went down at my place last we talked..."

"*Upset* is not the word and there's no *probably* about it."

"Okay, and I get it. I could have handled things way better than I did."

"You got that right."

"Which is why I'm calling now. I want to rectify things."

"Did you mean what you said about not wanting to be friends with me anymore?"

Stumped again. "Umm...Cam, I..."

"Yeah, that's what I thought," he scoffed. "Doesn't seem like there's much to rectify, then, does it?"

"Cam, please try to understand this from my side, and how hard this is for me. Of course the *last* thing I want to do is not have you in my life anymore. You mean the world to me, and that's not just my unrequited love talking."

He stayed quiet, though I'd hoped this was when he'd jump in and admit his feelings for me, too. But either he was too pissed at me to admit them or he didn't have them at all, which still stung to think about.

"Can you at all understand how difficult it is for me to be around you with these...these feelings knowing you'll probably never feel the same way?" I continued, choosing to just forge ahead. "And we both know that it's only a matter of time before you meet someone else and then that torture will start all over again. That would be tough for *anyone* to deal with, Cam."

"Well, clearly you have it all figured out," he replied, his voice holding no warmth whatsoever. I wasn't used to him speaking to me like this and I hated it. "I don't see what the point of us having this conversation was if you apparently know everything that's gonna happen."

"What else *could* happen, though, Cam? I mean, if I'm wrong, please tell me."

He was quiet for a few moments. "Do what you've gotta do, Nyla," he finally said. The emptiness in his voice sent an eerie chill through me. "Apparently you know what I think and feel better than I do, right? It's all about what *you* want; that's been established already. I told you I don't wanna lose you, and I don't, but that didn't matter. Then you ignored me for days. So excuse me if I'm a little fed up and not in the mood to try to plead my case again for nothing."

"Oh." I sniffed, the tears already running. It was like I could *hear* my heart breaking. "Okay, then."

"Are we done?"

Sounds like it. "I guess."

He hung up.

It didn't take long for me to start freaking out. Which of course sent me running to Sleek and bothering Kori in the middle of the workday.

"I know it's Saturday and you're really busy but I need to talk and I can't wait hours until you get off," I spewed as soon as we were behind the door of her small, cramped office.

"It's fine; that's what employees are for," Kori assured me, gently guiding me to the lone chair in front of her slightly-messy desk. "We've got a few minutes. What's going on?"

"I called Cam," I announced. "It did *not* go well."

"Oh no. What happened?"

I recalled the conversation with Cam, which of course brought the tears again. "He was just *over* it," I finished, taking the tissue Kori handed me. "There was no hashing anything out or coming to any kind of compromise..."

"What kind of compromise could you have come to, though, Nyla? Did you want him to agree to not see anyone else until you got past your feelings for him?"

"That never even crossed my mind. Not that I'd ask him to do that."

"Exactly. Like he said, your mind was already made up. Honestly, what could he have said – other than 'Nyla, I'm in love with you, too' – that would have made any difference?"

"I don't know, Kori. I didn't have a script for this. I just know I didn't expect for him to be so cold. He's *never* talked to me like that before, never. And we've had some big arguments. But I've never wondered if I'd ever hear from him again like I do now. For all I know, he's deleted my number and is trying to forget he ever knew me."

"I seriously doubt that." Kori actually chuckled, like any of this was funny. "Cam isn't done with you, girl."

"Believe me, Kori, you didn't hear him."

"I didn't have to hear him to be sure about this one. And yeah, I might not know Cam as well as you do, but I know men pretty well. He's hurt and pissed and trying to protect *his* feelings now."

My head snapped up. That hadn't even occurred to me. "You think?"

"I'm telling you. Whatever Cam felt for you before, it hasn't gone anywhere."

"That's reassuring. That's better to believe than what's in my head right now."

"This is just a case of a bruised ego that needs time to heal, that's all. He's feeling this just like you are. But I will say that the anger over you sticking to ending your friendship will probably be there for a while. I could see if you were walking that back but you weren't, so..."

"I'm getting that *you're taking his side more than you are mine* vibe again."

"Just telling it like it is. I told you I get where you're coming from but I definitely get his side, too."

"Yeah, well..." I sighed. "I'm already starting to regret all of this, regardless of why I started it. I don't want to lose Cam, Kori. As a friend or anything else."

"I know you don't, girl. Maybe you need something else to focus on."

"I've been redecorating the apartment. Spending money I have no business spending."

"Fun, but I was thinking of something with a penis."

She actually laughed at how my jaw dropped. "Excuse me?"

"Let me set you up."

"Oh no," I quickly protested, shaking my head and finger in unison. "I don't wanna be set up."

"Why? Because you're still pining over Cam? Girl, I'm trying to help you get over that. Maybe you can rekindle your friendship with him if you catch feelings for someone else."

"I'm not jerking Cam around like that. 'Oh, I don't think we should talk unless I happen to fall for somebody else?' That's not fair to him."

"Okay fine, forget about the Cam part of it for a second, then. I can set you up just because. You haven't met anyone new in a while. And now that you've finally stopped going back and forth with Kendrick, it's about time you met someone new."

"No, thanks. And before you lecture me, it has nothing to do with me pining over Cam. I'm not holding out for him to change his mind or declaring myself off men. I'm just not desperate for anything. Really, if I meet someone naturally and we hit it off, great. But-"

"You mean like the way you and Cam met?"

"Thanks for reminding me of that. But yes."

"If you say so. Do your thing, then. I need to get back out there but I'll say this again in case you forgot; Cam isn't done with you. Mark my words."

I wasn't sure if I believed that but damn it, I couldn't help but hope it was true.

"Nyla, I hate to be the bearer of bad news first thing in the morning."

I hadn't even had coffee yet. Turning in my seat, I forced a pleasant-enough smile as I looked up at Zack. "Might as well get it over with. What, I didn't get the promotion?"

He looked genuinely remorseful as he shook his head. I blew out a breath, processing the news.

"I don't suppose they mentioned why?" I finally asked.

"All I got was the empty corporate PC talk about them going with someone they felt was more suited for the position. So I'm sure one of their friends or little protégés will be announced as the new manager soon. It's such bull."

I agreed but wasn't about to say it out loud. "Well, that's too bad. I really thought I had a shot."

"You *should* have had one," Zack insisted. "I tried to tell them they should reconsider but their minds were made up. This is part of the reason I'm moving on from here; the way they do things is...ridiculous."

Right again. "In any case, I appreciate you going to bat for me, even though it turned out to be for nothing. When is your last day?"

"Another week. And between you and me, I can't wait. I promised to hang around until they found my replacement so...now I can finally get out of here."

"We're gonna miss you around here." *Ehh*. "And thanks again for all of the support."

"No problem. I hope you find something even bigger and better."

"Thanks, Zack."

He went on about his business and I tried to decide just how upset I was about not getting that promotion to manager. It was a strange mix of wanting to be chosen but not actually wanting the position, yet still feeling slighted by not getting it. I cared about the raise that came with the job more than the job itself.

Still, though, I found myself feeling a little bummed. And since word got around in our office like a virus, it didn't take long at all for several people to either come to my desk, email, instant message, or stop me in the halls to say how sorry they were that I was passed over. It was all very nice but making it very difficult for me to forget I ever tried for the damn promotion.

Add in the fact that I'd lost my favorite berry lip gloss, and I was having a pretty crappy Monday.

Maybe it was time to make my own move, away from BryCom. I'd gotten comfortable there but was just going through the motions. I didn't love it; it was just a job. Which would've been fine if I was at least raking in the dough there but that wasn't the case, either.

And looking for a better-suited job would help keep my mind off of you-know-who.

I'd been hoping he'd call. Or at least text. That he'd calm down and miss me so much that he'd find any random reason to reach out to me. Maybe he'd find a pen or something that I'd left at his place and need to return it.

Maybe it wasn't fair to wish for that after cutting him off like I did but damn, did I miss him already. I didn't know how the *hell* I was going to manage this, going on without Cam. He'd only been in my life for a year and some change but I still couldn't imagine him not being there for me.

Oh well. I'd made this bed, so I had to lie in it.

I trudged through the rest of the workday, looking forward to sprucing up my resume and hitting all the job sites when I got home. And my neighbor Jenny was supposed to call me when the furniture she ordered came in; I'd helped her choose a vibe and color scheme and narrow things down, because she was all over the place, wanting some of everything. And that overwhelmed her, which is why she ended up choosing nothing. She got so excited when I helped her that she went ahead and paid me a hundred bucks just for that one 'consultation.' I thought it was too much but I wasn't stupid enough to turn it down. That was gas and grocery money right there.

Finally, the end of the workday came. I yawned as I gathered my things and headed out to my car.

"Have a good night, Nyla."

"Thanks, you too." I didn't even know who it was I was talking to; I just kept walking.

I unlocked the door to my car, yanking it open and tossing my purse and laptop bag in. I frowned curiously then exhaled in relief when I noticed the tube of berry lip gloss under the driver's seat; I'd been looking for that for days. It must have fallen out of my pocket.

I was fishing for it when Kori called.

"Heading home?" she asked once I finally dug the phone from my pocket and answered it.

"I will be in a minute."

"What's wrong? You sound like you've had a day."

"Ehh. You could say that. It's about time for me to find another job."

"What??" she gasped. "Did you get laid off?"

"No, nothing like that. I didn't get that promotion, though."

"Oh, damn. Girl, I'm sorry."

"It is what it is." I grunted in frustration as I accidentally pushed the lip gloss further under the seat instead of grabbing it.

"What are you doing?"

"Ugh, nothing. But anyway, I figured it's just time for a change, that's all. I have a feeling that this is probably as high as I'm gonna get at BryCom and I'd rather not be stuck in this same position for the next ten years."

"It's about time. I've been wondering when you were going to finally break outta there."

"Yeah. So, I'm gonna start seeing what I can find."

"Do you know what you wanna do? I'll certainly keep my ear to the ground, too."

"Still figuring that part out."

"Understandable. So...I'm sure you know I'm gonna ask..."

"No, I haven't talked to Cam." My frown deepened.

"Damn. I was hoping maybe he called."

You and me both. "No."

"You holding up okay? I know you're probably missing him like crazy."

I was, but instead of admitting it, I just bit my lip and zeroed in on my mission of grasping the lip gloss under my seat, trying to go in under the front instead of the side, but my hand wouldn't fit. Back to the side.

"Nyla?"

"I'm here..."

"Did you hear what I said?"

"Yeah. Just got a little distracted. Um, you don't have to keep bringing up Cam. If the miracle of him calling happens, you know I'll tell you."

"I just know this is tough on you. You don't have to try to act like it isn't."

I felt that ache that came with the reality of the decision I made to detach myself from Cam. I'd managed to suppress it most of the day, but now it was front and center in my mind again. Great.

"It is, but...I need to find a way to move past it, like I'm sure Cam has."

"I'd bet anything that he's no more past it than you are. He's probably miserable, just like you. And if you're starting to rethink your decision, I'm sure he'd be glad to hear it."

"Hmph. I don't know about all that."

"I do."

When I finally grabbed the lip gloss tube, I tried to pull my hand back out but of course my sleeve got caught on one of the little metal bars under the seat. I pulled, hating that I was probably going to have a big snag in my sweater sleeve. After a few tries, I decided I didn't care about snags and just tried to yank my hand out.

"Nyla?"

"I'm here..."

"What's going on?"

"Nyla, you okay?" I heard someone call from nearby. I glanced over and it was Zack, who was standing next to his Jeep. "Is your hand stuck or something?"

"Kinda but I've got it," I insisted, feeling a little foolish.

"You sure you don't need some help?"

"Oh, no...thanks, though." My cheeks flushed as I turned my face away and gave one more hard yank, succeeding finally in freeing my hand.

Unfortunately, the upward momentum sent my hand smacking hard against the doorframe. I screeched in pain, forgetting to back up before shooting upright, and banged my head against the doorframe's hard rim. A searing pain ripped through my head as I winced and dropped the phone, then fell down next to it.

"Nyla!"

Chapter 13

I heard voices, but I didn't know whose they were. Then I heard one that I'd know anywhere.

"I can take her home now?"

"Yes, we've concluded that she doesn't have a concussion. But she should still take it easy and get plenty of rest."

"Oh, I'll make sure of that, believe me. She won't lift a finger."

Where did Cam come from?

Or was I dreaming?

Ooh, was this one of those times like in the movies where you wish for something enough and it manifests like a sexy-scented cloud? Because I definitely smelled cologne.

Then the voice I didn't recognize said something about discharge papers and staying with me for at least a day to keep an eye on me. Cam's voice said he wouldn't leave my side.

I opened my eyes on my bed at home, but I was still fuzzy on how I ended up there. I vaguely remembered leaving work and talking to Kori, but that was it.

"How you feeling?"

Cam appeared in my bedroom doorway with a mug in his hand, looking concerned. I noted his brick red sweater with the sleeves pushed up and showing some sexy forearms, and dark jeans.

"What happened?" I croaked, then immediately cleared my throat. I moved to sit up and Cam quickly came over to help me.

"You hit your head in the parking lot at work."

"I did?"

"Yeah. Apparently you were out for a minute."

"I don't even remember that..."

"Which is exactly why I'm not leaving here until I'm sure you're good." He handed me the mug of what smelled like hot apple cider and looked at me, gently sitting beside me on the bed. "You *do* know who I am, right?"

"Cuba Gooding Jr.?"

"Oh hell; where did I put that doctor's number??"

"Cam, I'm kidding," I assured with a small smile, placing my free hand on his arm. "Of course I know who you are."

"Don't play with me like that." His mild frown melted back to the concerned expression he wore when he came in. "They said you don't have a concussion but that you might still be out of it. And that symptoms just might not have shown up yet."

"I'm sure I'm fine. But my head hurts..."

"I've got some Tylenol here. You need to eat something first, though."

"Whatever you say." I had no energy to protest. "How did you get here? I mean, how did...who told you-"

"The guy you work with, Zack," Cam informed. "When he saw you go down, he called me after getting you to the hospital. He still had my card from when we met at that office party thing you dragged me to."

"Oh yeah. He was rather fascinated by you."

"Which kinda freaked me out. I told him I just write about sports, I don't play 'em myself. But he kept popping up asking a bunch of questions. It was like he'd never seen an incredibly debonair Black brotha before. I know I'm wonderful and all..."

"Is comedy one of the methods they told you to use for my recovery?"

"Don't try to deny how hot I am. Anyway, he called me and I dropped everything and came to see about you."

"Oh Cam..."

"I need to let Kori know you're home, too...she was kinda freaking out. Zack had picked up your phone when you went down and she was still on there, screaming her head off, apparently. She was the only one at the store but was gonna close up and come to the hospital, but I got there first. I called her from your phone and told her I had you. I also told you her you need to rest and she can come see you tomorrow."

"Okay." I took a long sip of cider and reached to put the mug on the nightstand, and Cam quickly moved to do it for me. I gazed at him, my mind a confusing swirl of thoughts.

He noticed. "What's wrong?"

"I guess I can't believe you're really here."

"Why wouldn't I be?"

"Cam. I know I hit my head but I'm pretty sure we had a falling out a few days ago. And you were majorly upset with me."

"So what? Just because I'm pissed at you doesn't mean I stop caring, Nyla. And there was no way I was going to hear about you being in the hospital and not get my ass over there to you. When Zack told me you hit your head and was knocked out..." He paused, swallowing as his eyes dropped to my hand on the bed between us. A beat passed before he firmly grasped it in his. "It scared me. More than I've been in a while."

This wasn't helping me get over my love for him.

But for the time being, I didn't care about that. I was just thankful and thrilled that he was there.

"Thank you, Cam," I whispered, squeezing his hand. "Thank you for being here."

"I wouldn't be anywhere else." He looked up at me, his eyes roaming mine. His mouth opened to say something, but he apparently thought better of it.

Neither of us said anything for a few moments, and I could almost feel the vibe shift around us. Cam suddenly seemed nervous, darting his eyes to me then looking away. I noticed he kept clenching his jaw, too.

"I'll, um...I'll get you something to eat," he finally said. "I can see what you have in the kitchen or order something."

"Whichever. I'm not even sure what's in the fridge. Either way, you know what I like."

"That I do." He stood, reluctantly releasing my hand. "I'll get the Tylenol, too."

"I appreciate it."

Cam ended up ordering some Chinese food, which we ate on my bed. I wanted to turn on the television but he wasn't having it, saying the mental stimulation was a no-no. So we just ate and talked and played too many games of Rock-Paper-Scissors (not sure why), betting stuff we both knew we weren't going to collect on. Then he rubbed my feet until I dozed off, though he'd wake me every so often to make sure I was all right.

I woke up on my own a couple of hours later to go to the bathroom, and when I came back, I just stood and watched Cam sleep on the other side of my bed, fully-clothed, breathing deeply with the slightest frown on his face. Wonder what he was dreaming about.

Realizing I was still in my work clothes, I went to take a quick shower and do the rest of my nightly ablutions before popping another Tylenol and easing back into bed. I didn't worry too much about being gentle since Cam tended to sleep like a log, but as soon as my head hit the pillow, I heard his voice.

"Why didn't you tell me?"

There was no point in acting like I didn't know what he was talking about. I kept my back to him as I replied, "Too scared to."

"Too scared to tell me you loved me?"

"That I was *in* love with you, yes. Those aren't the same thing."

"I get that. But that's something I would have liked to know."

"Why? You were with Jada."

"I thought you said you've been in love with me since we met. That was long before Jada."

"Still, I..." Sighing, I momentarily closed my eyes. "Let's not do this."

I felt him move closer to me. My back was to him but I could feel his body heat.

"I want to do it."

Why did his voice have to drop when he said that? It was hard enough being on my bed with him and trying not to picture his body naked and oiled. I wasn't eager to add to the struggle by rehashing my one-sided feelings.

"Cam...go back to sleep."

"Why are you trying to avoid this?"

"Because there's no point. It was pointless to bring it up before and it's pointless to talk about now."

"I disagree." He placed a hand on my hip. "It's anything but pointless."

The warmth from his hand spread over my body like a wildfire and I hated the whimper that escaped before I could stop it. "Let's just leave well enough alone. You're here and I'm grateful for that; we don't have to rock the boat with anything else."

He was quiet for a few moments before his fingers flexed on my hip. "Look at me, Nyla."

I took my time doing it, but I eventually turned onto my back, looking at him in the darkened room. Moonlight through the sheer curtains on my window allowed me to see his face enough, and he moved closer and leaned over me, resting on his arm near my head. He looked right into my eyes, and I had to force myself to hold his gaze.

"Do you not believe I could love you back?" he finally asked. "The way you love me?"

His hand immediately but gently grabbed my chin and turned it back to him when I tried to look away.

"Answer me," he ordered, his voice tender.

"I-I don't know..."

"Yes, you do."

"I know I'm not your type. I've seen the kind of women you go for and that's *not* me."

"I'm in my thirties and you've known me a little over a year. That's not a large sample size, Nyla. Certainly not enough for you to just decide that on your own."

"You've never given any indication of attraction to me before. Not really."

"You're damn attractive. Anybody can see that. Just because I don't say it doesn't mean I'm not aware of it."

"If you're doing this to try to make me feel better or to appease my ego, you really don't have to."

"This has nothing to do with that. When have you known me to say shit I don't mean?"

He had me with that one.

"Regardless, I don't need any pity," I stubbornly proclaimed, folding my arms over my breasts. "I can't be mad at you for not feeling what I feel. It's fine. I'll learn to live with it. But let's not make things worse by-"

He stopped my yammering with his lips, leaning down to cover mine with his. Another whimper escaped as I immediately kissed him back, opening my mouth and accepting all the tongue he had for me. He palmed my face, his fingertips gripping the nape of my neck. I both hated and loved how I automatically responded to him.

"What are you doing?" I panted between kisses.

His body leaned in closer. "Kissing you."

"Cam...maybe we shouldn't..." My voice might've been trying to protest but my hand was gripping his shirt, keeping him close. "You don't have to do this."

He pulled away slightly, his eyes a mix of frustration and...something else. "Damn shame that you think that the only reason I'd kiss you is out of pity or obligation. And I know it's not 'cause you have low self-esteem."

"No, Cam, I'm..." My eyes dropped to my hand that was still gripping his shirt. "I'm just being realistic."

"Realistic, huh? Well, here's some realness for you. I *am* attracted to you, Nyla. Always was. You honestly think I never noticed how fucking cute you are?"

My cheeks were on fire.

"But when we met, *how* we met, I just veered towards the protective side than the romantic one," he continued. "You became *so* important to me, and I made it my job to look out for you. But when you came out the night me and Jada ultimately broke up, wearing that outfit with the shorts and the heels...I couldn't get it out of my head. I couldn't get *you* out of my head."

I'll be damned; Kori's advice actually worked.

"So I had to put on some booty shorts for you to notice me, huh?" I made myself scoff.

He shot me a look, fully aware of what I was trying to do. "It wasn't about the shorts, Nyla. It was a reminder. You're my best friend but you're also a sexy-ass woman. And it made me face up to the real reason I always got so upset when I saw you talking to other guys. I've had female friends before and while I cared about them, I never cared about who they dated as long as they were good dudes. But with you, it didn't matter *who* it was; I...I couldn't stand to see you with anybody else."

I swore I could hear my heart beating, the way it thumped in my chest. My breasts heaved slightly between us. "Really?"

"Really." His thumb stroked my cheek. "I love kissing you, Nyla."

Everything on my body clenched. It was the closest I've ever come to an orgasm just from a few words.

"Cam..."

"I love kissing you now just like I loved it the first time out on the couch that day."

It took a second for his words to register and when they did, my eyes widened. "What?"

"You heard me, Nyla. You asked me if I remembered the kiss from before and I do. The day you hurt your ankle and we got drunk and ate tacos."

"I...why didn't you say that when I asked you?"

"You were throwing a lot at me at once; I couldn't think straight. But of course I remembered it. It screwed my head up so much that I was confused, and started questioning everything. It's also how I knew I needed to stop messing around with Jada. She wasn't it for me."

I started to ask if I was when he leaned down and resumed our kiss, moaning and igniting my raging arousal even more. Something in me clicked and all my doubts vanished, at least for the time being.

"Remember how I got on top of you?" he whispered, sliding his body onto mine. He bit his bottom lip and looked over me hungrily. And believe me, I was looking at him the same way.

"Yes..."

"Remember how I moved?" His hips started grinding against me, and I almost lost it.

"*Fuck*, yes..." My hands slid to his ass, pulling him and matching his rhythm.

"Shit, Nyla..." He leaned up long enough to pull off his sweater. I'd seen his chest plenty of times before but having it on top of me where I could openly ogle and touch and graze his nipples with my nails was a whole different pleasure. "What are you doing to me right now?"

I responded by wrapping my legs around his waist, clamping us together. I hated that there were so many clothes between us.

"I've been *dreaming* about getting my hands back on these." His hand squeezed my breast before he started stroking his thumb back and forth across my nipple. I groaned in delicious frustration. "Wanting to do it again..."

"Under the shirt, Cam," I breathed, grabbing his wrist. "Touch me *under* the shirt."

"Oh, I can do better than that." He lifted my night shirt, grunting appreciatively when he found no bra. When he slid down slightly to tease my nipple with his tongue before sliding it into his mouth and sucking, I threw my head back and screamed. I didn't know if it was Cam's skills or technique or if it was just *Cam*, but it didn't matter. It felt too good.

Eventually my shirt was on the floor next to Cam's, and we spent the rest of the night fooling around and pleasuring each other on my bed. I wasn't even sure if that was something I was supposed to be doing in my condition, but there was no way I was stopping this pleasure train. I was already worried that this was some kind of dream I was about to wake up from.

But it wasn't. Cam was really there, in my bed, on top of me, just like I'd fantasized about so many times. And I was gonna enjoy the hell out of it.

I was in Bed Bath and Beyond trying to conquer the decision of ombre striped shower curtain or the one with the big pretty flower on it. They didn't look anything alike so I wasn't sure why these were even the finalists. I guess it was just easier to focus on something inane like this rather than obsess over what happened with Cam.

It had been three days since our night together and my mind was officially blown. And we didn't even have sex; it was just a *lot* of kissing and heavy petting (and licking and sucking and...*umph*) but that had been plenty. The morning after, there was no acting like it hadn't happened; he kissed me like a girlfriend and stayed the rest of the day to make sure no dormant concussion symptoms popped up, being more affectionate than ever. While I loved that he wasn't ignoring what happened, I couldn't help being a little freaked out.

So I was pretty relieved when Cam finally went home, even though there was the part of me that didn't want him to leave. I wanted more days of him doting on me and us talking and tripping out, and more nights in my bed.

At the same time, though, I didn't know where we stood, and it left my mind free to wander all over the place. Cam's actions might have indicated that things had changed between us, but we still hadn't talked about it. I felt we needed to but realized I wouldn't know what I'd say if we did.

"Screw it, I'll just get both of 'em," I finally muttered, grabbing both shower curtains. Totally different color schemes, which meant I'd need more coordinating towels and floor rugs. Cute toothbrush holders and soap dispensers. Baskets, shower caddies, an iron stand to hold extra rolls of toilet paper. I just kept loading things into my cart, barely looking at the prices.

It was easier to put energy into decking out my little bathroom than trying to figure out what was happening between me and Cam. At least this time, I was using a gift card I'd won at work instead of my own money.

A text from Cam came in when I pulled up at home and was getting my bags from the car, and it reminded me of him appearing like a knight when I hurt my ankle trying to carry a hundred things in by myself at once. I couldn't help but smile, remembering that.

I took my time checking Cam's text as I made three trips getting my things up to my apartment. I told myself that was learning my lesson from last time, but it was really more like stalling.

Once I got everything inside and took my time putting each item away, I finally forced myself to see what Cam had sent.

Wanna hang out tonight? I'm covering a game but can come over after. Miss you.

I missed him, too. But instead of doing the grown-woman thing and telling him that, I just replied:

I'll let you know ASAP. Is that ok?

His response came quickly.

Yeah, that's cool.

We're good, right?

Of course he could tell that something was off. He knew me way too well.

Yeah, totally fine.

I'm sure it was throwing him off that I had confessed to being in love with him and let him treat my body like a playground and now I was being all standoffish. There was no telling what he was thinking of me right then.

I wanted to call Kori but I knew she was working. So I grabbed my keys to go bother her in person.

"Hey!" She grinned as she stood from where she was rearranging some things on the bottom of one of the jewelry displays. She held her arm out for a hug as I went over to her. "I didn't know you were coming by here today."

"Yeah...just needed to get out of the house." I didn't bother mentioning that I was *in* the house all of maybe twenty minutes. I glanced around. "Slow period?"

"Girl, slow *day*." Kori sighed, shaking her head. "Only two customers since I opened."

"Oh no..."

"I'm not stressing, though...it happens," Kori quickly insisted, her bright smile returning. "This is how it goes sometimes; my mentor mamas said there'd be days like this."

"Where's Elsa?" I asked, referring to her sole employee.

"Errands. She should be back in a little while. So that means you have some time to tell me about whatever is going on with you and Cam."

I didn't even waste time trying to act startled. I just went in.

"Fine, so...Cam and I had this amazing time the other night and he seems like he wants to move forward and take things beyond friendship-"

"I think y'all crossed that bridge when y'all were hunching all night."

"Shut up. Anyway, I haven't really known what to say to him so I've been keeping him at arms-length, though I think he's starting to catch on."

"Why wouldn't he? The man isn't stupid."

"Kori."

"What I don't understand is why you're not over the moon about all this," she replied, going back to resume her jewelry arranging. "You've wanted this man forever. Now he's finally seeing you as more than a friend and you're *still* not satisfied?"

"It's not that I'm not satisfied, it's just...I don't know how to explain it. The other night was...amazing. And most of me is thrilled that he seems to be as attracted to me as I am to him."

"But..."

"But now I'm wondering how things will be between us from here on out. You know everything changes when you get physical."

"You wanted that, though. Some change is good. And necessary."

"But sometimes it *isn't*," I countered. "Sometimes things are better off staying how they are."

"You are making *no* sense. You were ready to end your friendship because you thought he didn't reciprocate your feelings for him. Yet he *still* came running when you were in the hospital and stayed by your side. Then he admitted that he doesn't just see you as a friend like you thought he did. Now you're talking about things don't need to change?"

"Well! It makes sense if you *really* think about it..."

"No it does not, Nyla." She stood up and looked at me pointedly, one of those arched brows at attention. "Look, it's just the two of us in here. Why don't you stop playing and just be real about what it is?"

"I-I don't know what it is you want me to say."

"Yes the hell you do. I always keep it real with you so don't you dare lie to me. Don't insult me with this bullshit."

"Fine, I'm scared, all right!" I glanced around even though I knew it was just us there. "I'm scared that if me and Cam jump into this thing and try to go deep, everything will just sink to the bottom and die. I'm scared that what makes him love me so much as a friend won't translate if I'm his girlfriend. I'm scared that the reality won't match the fantasy."

The anger in her eyes softened when she saw the tears welling in mine. I don't know if *I* even realized that's what my problem was until that moment.

"I *want* him, Kori," I assured, meaning it more than I've ever meant anything. "But if it doesn't work out-"

"See, that? You have to stop that," Kori interjected, coming over to me with a pointed finger. She looked down at me with the empathy I needed right then. "Don't crash the car before you've even put it in drive."

"I'm not trying to be pessimistic."

"You're trying to justify not trying. And I'm telling you, you will regret it if you don't. None of us can predict the future and I'm not gonna stand here and declare that you and Cam will be forever 'cause I don't know that. But my point is, *you don't know that you* won't, *either*."

"Damn it," I whispered, using both hands to wipe my eyes before running them through my hair. "I'm really messing this up."

"Yeah." She pulled me in for a hug. "You are. Now quit being a punk and get your man."

Chapter 14

Ms. Nelson,

Thank you for your interest in the Supervisor position. We'd love to have you come in for an interview.

Good afternoon Ms. Nelson,

We were very intrigued by your cover letter and resume. Would you be able to come in for an interview next week?

Ms. Nelson,

We're still narrowing our search for the position of Office Supervisor and are very interested in speaking more with you. We have some available times for interviews below; please let us know which one works for you.

"Wow, *three* interview requests?"

I was a little surprised to see the requests in my inbox wanting me to come interview. This was what I should have expected from sending out my resume but apparently I had it in my head that that was as far as it would go. My resumes would just be floating in the digital atmosphere for eternity, forever ignored.

Even though I applied for these positions, I was tempted to ignore these interview requests and just stay at BryCom. Way easier than starting over somewhere new. As for the money issue, I could always just ask for a raise. Maybe they'd give me that, since they passed over me for that promotion.

Wait, what am I doing??

I could hear Kori's voice in my head telling me to quit looking for the easy way out. But I still wasn't hyped at the thought of taking another office job. Yes, I needed to take a step forward. I wasn't trying to look up in five years and still be in the same position at BryCom. Especially since I didn't even really like the job that much.

But...office supervisor? Again? How is *that* a step forward? It was pretty much same shit, different toilet.

So I closed my email and played a few games of Bejeweled.

Cam was banging on my door. I knew he'd show up sooner or later.

"What's the deal, Nyla? Why are we here again?"

I closed the door behind him and nervously slid my hands into my back pockets. He looked understandably upset.

"Cam, I'm sorry." It was the only thing I could say.

"Yeah?" He crossed his arms over his chest. "Just so I'm clear, what exactly is it that you're sorry *for*?"

"For..." I hunched my shoulders. "Being scared. And not knowing what I'm doing."

"In regards to what? Me?"

"You...us...hell, everything. I'm just a little overwhelmed."

"I really don't get you." He shook his head. "Why the hell did you ever tell me about your feelings for me if you didn't really want to do anything about them?"

Good question. "It's not that I don't want to do anything about them; it's just that when it came time to, it just got so...so *real* and I didn't know how to handle it."

"And you did what you always do and hid from it instead of facing it and figuring it out, like a *grown* woman would."

I recoiled as if he slapped me because that's sure what it felt like. "Damn, Cam, really?"

"Well, excuse me that I'm not in the mood to spare your feelings right now, 'cause you surely haven't given much of a damn about mine lately. In fact, you have a history of just deciding that you don't wanna be bothered with me and you back the fuck off, and I'm just supposed to deal with it. But let me do the same thing to you and I'd be all kinds of jacked up."

"Okay, you're not wrong about that..."

"You tell me you love me, then instead of giving me time to respond, you kick me out. We have a great night together where I *thought* we came to a mutual understanding *finally*, and then you basically ghost me. I mean, what the hell??"

"I know..."

"And if I hadn't come over here now, there's no telling *when* we'd talk. I love you, Nyla, you know that. But this is getting old. How much of this am I supposed to put up with?"

"Cam, I..." I stepped over to him, fear running through me at his words. As much as I'd said before that I wasn't sure I needed to keep Cam around, it was different to hear him hint at the same thing. "I get it; I can be frustrating to deal with. I get in my own head and my own feelings and don't know how to handle it."

"You run when things get tough." His voice was as strong as his statement. "Let's just call it what it is."

"Wow," I whispered, my eyes dropping to the floor for a second. "I, um...that's hard to hear but I guess I can't deny it."

"You *say* you want things but when it comes time to actually go for it, you punk out."

"I get it, Cam. And you're right; I know that."

"Nyla," He took a step towards me. "What is it you're afraid of?"

"I..." *Just spit it out, girl; you owe it to him to be honest.* "I'm afraid of things not being like I've imagined. With me and you, I mean. I've been crushing on you for so long and picturing all of these things in my head..."

"What, that if I don't live up to your fantasies, everything will be ruined? You'll feel like wanting me was a waste?"

"No! Well, not exactly..."

"Nyla, I'm here." He grabbed my hand, putting it on his chest. "I'm right here. I'm a real, human man who can't read your mind or see what's in your head. If you just want to live off of your fantasies, let me know now. But if you want to see where it can go with the real thing..." He held my wrist with both hands and looked hopefully into my eyes, "I'm here. And I *wanna* be here but you have to trust me."

Everything in me wanted to jump into his arms. Because I wanted him no less than I always did.

"And you're sure you're over Jada?"

His face went from surprised to confused to angry in a matter of seconds.

"Are you fuckin' kidding me right now??" he exclaimed, dropping my hand. "I come to you on some real shit and tell you I want to be with you and you're worried about my *ex*?"

Momentarily stumped, I made myself shake it off. "I have every right to wonder about that, Cam!"

"Why is that? We weren't married. I wasn't in love with her. I barely called her my girlfriend. And you see I haven't mentioned her since I told you that my feelings for you were part of the reason she and I split. So there's really *no* reason for you to wonder about that."

"Can you not understand why I'd be a little bit skeptical with all this? During our entire friendship you've seen me one way and now suddenly you're seeing me as another?"

"So, what, you don't trust me?"

"I didn't say that."

"It can be what you meant without you saying the words verbatim. You're basically saying I'm full of shit."

"Don't put words in my mouth, Cam."

"I wish I could, 'cause the ones that are coming *out* of your mouth are pissing me off."

"I'm sorry, I thought we were being real with each other. I thought our friendship was strong enough to withstand a little candor."

"Oh you want candor? I *got* your candor. I don't think you know *what* the fuck you want, Nyla. No matter what I say to you, you'll try to find some new problem or reason to run from it, justifying the hell out of it to yourself so you don't have to actually try anything. What excuse are you gonna come up with next, huh?"

"It's not like I'm *trying* to come up with excuses, Cam. I *do* still love you. I *do* still want to be with you."

"Well, I can't tell that. 'Cause to me it seems like you're doing everything possible to push me away."

"I'm not...damn, can you just give me a little time? Can't you just be patient? I just told you what I want but...don't I deserve some time to...be ready?"

He stood up a little straighter as he looked at me, his jaw clenching. I knew he was frustrated with me (I was frustrated with myself) but we could work this out. Even if we took the slow walk towards where we were both trying to go. Thankfully, I knew Cam loved me enough to indulge me this.

Which is why I was totally surprised when he finally responded.

"No."

I blinked. "What?"

"No, I'm not giving you any time and my patience is *gone*, Nyla. Because I don't think you *want* to be ready. You just want to sit around and dream and wish instead of going for what you want. And I deserve better than that, since we're talking about what we *deserve* and all."

He turned to leave and my heart dropped to my stomach. I ran over to grab his arm before he could reach for the doorknob.

"Cam, please don't leave!"

"What am I staying for, Nyla? You're either too scared to really do this or you're playing games. Either way, I don't have time for it."

"I'm sorry! Cam, I...I'm absolutely not playing games; I wouldn't do that to you."

"So you're scared, then."

"Yes! I *am* scared, Cam! This...this is a lot! And as much as I *ache* to be with you, it freaks me out to think about it not working and you not being in my life anymore."

"Well stop thinking about that." He turned to face me and grabbed my shoulders before sliding his hands up to my neck, stroking my new tears with his thumbs. "Stop assuming everything is gonna fall apart. Some relationships *do* last."

"But none of the ones you've been in since I've met you have," I hesitantly countered. My hands rested lightly on his stomach. "It's just hard to imagine that I would be any different."

"You're already different." He leaned down and rested his forehead on mine. "I didn't have with any of them what I have with you. Hell, I've *never* had a friendship like this with another woman. You already mean the world to me. I need you to believe that I want this, Nyla. And that I'd never intentionally do anything to hurt you or lose you."

He kissed my forehead, then my nose, then both cheeks, slowly and deliberately. My eyes fluttered closed as my hands gripped his shirt.

"I *do* believe that..."

"Then I need you to have some faith in me. In *this*, in us. Let's just be together and enjoy it." He kissed my lips and pulled me closer, looking right into my eyes. "Or should I just leave now and we can act like none of this ever happened?"

I leaned up and claimed his lips, immediately stroking my tongue against his. In that moment I realized how dumb I was being, letting my fears almost make the man I've wanted for over a year walk out the door.

Cam fervently returned my kiss, one hand holding the back of my head and the other gripping my waist. I couldn't get close enough to him, and my hands tugged on the waistband of his jeans before opting to start pushing his shirt up his chest. He finished the job, pulling it over his head and tossing it aside as I yanked my own shirt off, then we went for each other's jeans. Once we were both in nothing but lotion, he came for my lips again, grabbing the backs of my thighs and lifting me. My legs wrapped his waist and my arms clamped around his neck as he backed me against the door, our kiss getting deeper and sloppier, our pants and moans and lip smacks taking up all the space.

"Here," he panted, holding up the condom he must have retrieved from his pocket during the brief moment I was trying to free my ankle from my pants leg. "Put it on me."

This wasn't my strong suit but I wasn't about to ruin the moment by admitting that. I temporarily brought my feet back to the floor so I could roll the condom on, and I must have done it right since he yanked me back up again as soon as I was done.

"You want this?" he grunted, sucking hard on my neck. That would surely leave a mark but that's what turtlenecks or scarves were for. "Tell me you want me, Nyla; I need to hear you say it."

I knew we weren't just talking about the sex. Pulling back slightly and grabbing his face with both hands, I looked straight into his eyes.

"Yes, Cam. I want you. In every way."

"You got me."

He licked my chin, making me shudder. I boldly eased my tongue out and touched it to his, starting a super-erotic tease that had me wetter than the Nile. He finally reached down and slid it in me, and I let out some sound I didn't have time to be embarrassed about. It just felt so amazing that my voice was doing its own thing.

"Ahhhh," Cam breathed, making his own noises as he briefly closed his eyes and let his head fall back. Then he looked at me and bit his bottom lip, and started stroking deeper. "Damn, baby..."

My arousal surged at the term of endearment, and my grip on him tightened. "Cam...*yes*, Cam..."

I held on for dear life as he sexed me against the front door, bracing my back against it as I rolled my hips against his, the pace increasing at a deliciously steady rate. My moans and screams increased with the rhythm, and I knew anybody walking by outside would be able to hear. Not that I gave a damn.

Cam leaned in for another kiss before we both looked down to watch our bodies joined together, the sight spurring both of us on. Pretty soon he was hitting it so hard that my back was banging against the door, and it was the kind of pain-pleasure that I'd only read about in the erotic novels I used to hide under my mattress.

"Shit!" I yelled, holding onto Cam tightly as he sexed me like he was punishing me. Hell, maybe he was. If this was how he was going to scold me, then I needed to think of some more ways to piss him off.

"You like it, huh?" he panted into my ear, his lips grazing my earlobe. "I *love* how wet you are for me."

"And I love how hard you are for me."

"So we gon' quit playin', right?" He braced a hand on the door over my head, his thrusts deepening and knocking my jaw slack. "It's you and me?"

"You...and...me," I managed to reply, my voice shaking as I felt the orgasm start to build. My nails dug into his shoulders. "Harder; I'm coming..."

With a loud grunt, he obliged my wish, giving me everything he had to the point where I knew I'd likely have bruises on my back later. Didn't care. Cam was living up to every nighttime (and daytime) sexual fantasy I'd ever had about him.

Suddenly I seized up, the orgasm hitting my body like a sexual taser. My eyes widened and my clamp on Cam tightened even more.

"Yeah, hold onto me," he urged, still stroking. "And I hope you're not done. 'Cause I plan on making up for a *lot* of lost time."

"You tryin' to wear me out?" I breathed, managing to smile before an aftershock hit me, causing me to bite my lip and release a long moan.

"Hell yeah."

In that moment, I would've agreed to anything. I wanted Cam on the floor, on the counter, on the couch, in my bed, in the shower, on the washing machine...not that I had one of those in my apartment, but still. I surely wished I did because I'd heard some great things about sex during the spin cycle.

After our door romp, we took it to my bedroom where we kicked things back up, this time with me getting reacquainted with Cam's body and exploring all of the sexiness up close. I felt like a newbie who'd just gotten their first hit, because I was definitely hooked and craving more.

"Now that we're both thinking straight," he said once we finally peeled ourselves off of each other, him holding me from behind and lightly running his lips up and down the back of my neck, "I'm gonna ask you again; it's you and me, right? Like, for real?"

I turned in his arms, facing him. Looking right into those adorable eyes of his, I replied, "For real. You and me."

His arms tightened around me. "You trust me, Nyla?"

"I do. I really do."

"And I can trust *you*?"

Mildly surprised by the question, I nodded. "Of course."

"That's what I needed to hear. I want this to work."

"Me, too."

"I know one thing," he said, trailing a finger between my breasts with a smirk. "I had no idea you were such a freak."

Laughing loudly, I playfully pushed his shoulder. "Shut up, you like it."

"Oh, I love it." He began to gently roll my nipple between his fingers, making me sharply draw in a breath.

"Yeah? Prove it, then."

"Oh, is that a challenge?" He pushed me onto my back and mounted me. "'Cause I don't lose those."

"That's what I'm counting on."

Chapter 15

So Cam was my man now.

It still felt surreal to even say that. What I've wanted for so long has finally happened and I could only pray to God that it wasn't some extremely realistic dream. I'd been pinching myself plenty to make sure.

It took a little getting used to, though. Whenever he called me 'baby' or anything like that, it actually jolted me like someone was pricking me with a pin, not to mention making me blush like a schoolgirl. It took a couple of weeks before I felt comfortable giving him a pet name, but he finally and officially reached Cammy Bae status. (He doesn't love that but still lets me say it).

We used to hang out a good bit when we were just friends but now, we were together basically every night. I was getting hooked on his company and his body and his touch and just *him*, and I didn't hate it at all. Yeah, there was still a little part of me that wanted to freak out by how fast things were moving, but mostly, I finally talked myself into just enjoying it.

"Where does this go?" Cam asked as he hauled a large Ficus plant through the door.

"You can just put it in the hallway for now. I'm still figuring out how I want to rearrange everything."

"You've got that bedroom looking *nice*, baby. That color you picked makes it look way bigger than it is."

"You mean white?" I asked with a chuckle.

"You tryin' to clown?" He grabbed my waist, tickling me.

"Cam, stop!" I laughed, trying to squirm away. "You *know* I'm ticklish!"

"Of course I know. Since you're trying to be funny, I figure you might as well be laughing."

"Ugh, I can't stand you sometimes."

"You love it. But for real, I dig the blue accent wall, and the new mirrors you got."

"I appreciate that. I so wish I could afford some of Dorian Clarke's pieces to put in here. I love stalking his Instagram page and website to drool over his stuff. Kori and I call him Furniture God."

"Yeah, you talk about him a lot. If I didn't know better, I'd be jealous."

"No need to be. I want his furniture, that's all. Oh, and thanks for doing most of the painting, since my short ass can hardly reach anything and I don't trust myself on ladders."

"You know I got you." He winked, chuckling. "Guess all that HGTV you watch did some good."

"I've always enjoyed this kind of stuff, anyway. It's fun to take an ordinary room and turn it into something you love being in."

"Where'd you get the idea to do your closet door like that? It legit looks like one of those French doors."

"Oh, I saw a tutorial online. It was pretty easy; just some painting and some gluing and voila. I highjacked Kori's backyard to do that and some other DIY stuff; saves me a few bucks."

"Like this dresser?" He pointed to the dresser that was still partially covered with a dropcloth.

"Oh, yeah. One of my neighbors was actually about to toss that so I snagged it; I needed a bigger one, anyway. I just sanded it, repainted it and replaced the handles. Good as new."

"Baby, you ever think about doing this for a living?" He looked at me, impressed. "You seem to have a knack for it and it's clearly something you're hyped about."

I hunched a shoulder. "I do love it but I honestly never considered really doing anything with it. It's more of a hobby."

"Plenty of successful businesses start out that way. And didn't you re-do your neighbor's place?"

"Oh, Jenny? Yeah, I helped her with her living room."

"And? Did she love it?"

"She's sent me like two dozen cupcakes on top of the money she paid me. So, yeah."

"Exactly my point, baby. Think how many more people you could probably bless in this building alone. You can't tell me that you wouldn't love doing that more than sitting in that dry-ass office at BryCom."

"Can't argue with you there."

"It's something to think about. That's all I'm saying."

I couldn't say I wasn't intrigued. Redecorating and design was fun for me, even the DIY stuff I did. Of course it was easier to just go out and buy stuff, but repurposing allowed me to be creative. And it was cool to make things that nobody else had.

Maybe that was something to think about. I still hadn't responded to those interview requests in my inbox, mostly because I felt they were just lateral moves; even if they paid a little more than I was making at BryCom, I'd still be doing something similar to what I was already doing. And that didn't excite me at all.

"Thanks for the suggestion, Cammy Bae," I grinned, winking at him.

"Ugh." He playfully rolled his eyes and pulled me to him, diving for my neck and making me giggle. "I'm gonna need you to come up with a better name than that."

"Why? It's cute, like you are."

"Yeah?" He kissed my lips. "How cute am I?"

"Quit trying to get me to hype you up."

"Hell, if I can't depend on my woman to hype me, who can?"

"Touché. Okay, well..." I slid my hands up his chest and looked up at the ceiling as if I had to think hard about this. "I'd say you're cuter than all the babies and all the puppies and-"

"This isn't really the direction I was thinking about..."

"And any of those bums they have on those Most Sexiest-whatever lists."

"That's more like it."

"Hey," I turned on my sex eyes as I grabbed his hands and pulled him backwards further into my bedroom. "Wanna christen the refurbished room now that the paint fumes are gone?"

Now *he* had the sex eyes. "You're reading my mind 'cause I was damn sure gonna suggest the same thing. The room isn't finished, though."

"Oh, we can do it again when it is. Call this a pre-christening."

"Girl, I love the way you think." He yanked me to him, taking the kiss he wanted. I *loved* when he got aggressive like that.

So we got it in on the floor of my bedroom (twice) before going to get something to eat. I was riding high, unable and unwilling to wipe the goofy smile off my face as Cam and I walked hand-in-hand to the restaurant. I'm sure my post-coital glow was evident but I didn't care.

"You know what you want?" Cam asked me after we were seated at our favorite hole-in-the-wall sports bar, perusing the menu.

"I want everything. I've barely eaten anything today and I'm starving."

"Yet you get onto me when I do that."

"I know, I know."

I saw a pretty woman heading our way that had legs I could only wish for, and my smile dimmed a little bit.

Please don't let her be our server, please don't let her be our server...

"Hi, I'm Kelly, and I'll be your server this evening."

Damn it.

"Hey, Kelly," Cam immediately greeted, glancing at her with a smile. I tried to gauge the length/appropriateness ratio.

"Hi," I felt obliged to say.

She flashed me a smile as she put some silverware rolled in napkins on the table. Her skin was the color of a shiny new penny. "I can get you two started on drinks. What would you like?"

"Beer," Cam and I answered in unison.

"Whatever's on tap is good," Cam added.

"No problem. Do you know what you'd like to order or do you need another minute?"

"We're ready. Let me get fifty wings, half lemon pepper, half teriyaki, fried hard." He looked at me. "You want some fries, babe?"

"Come on, now."

"Large order of fries," Cam told Kelly. "And lots of ranch dressing."

"Coming right up." She strutted off to the back and I eyed Cam to see if he'd watch her, even a little bit. He did glance as she walked away but it was only for a second.

"We're some greedy asses," I joked, shaking my head. "Whose gonna eat all that?"

"We will. If not here, then later on in my bed."

"Just don't be trying to keep me up all night. You know I have to get up earlier than you."

"Call in sick."

"Don't tempt me."

We continued to sit there trading our usual banter while we waited for our food. Cam casually held my hand on the table, at times glancing at a basketball game playing on one of the televisions mounted throughout the bar. I didn't care about that. But when his eyes would stray to one of the pretty servers roaming around...*that* I cared about.

To be fair, he wasn't ogling any of them. But his little looks *did* last a couple seconds too long, in my opinion. What was he looking at them for at all, anyway? I couldn't help but wonder if he thought they were hotter than me, but I knew asking him that would only start an argument.

I hated this paranoid side of myself that had to question everything. Cam was with *me*, holding *my* hand and playfully kicking *my* feet under the table. He'd just made love to *me* after spending his off day helping me redecorate my bedroom. Not to mention, he had assured me many times that I was who he wanted to be with. I didn't know why I couldn't just be confident in that.

But at least this time, I was keeping my mouth shut about it.

A couple of days later, I was sitting at my makeshift desk in Jada's old room (which was next on my list to redecorate), looking over some information for interior design classes. Ever since Cam had suggested that as a career path, I hadn't been able to get it out of my mind. The more I thought about it, the more excited I got, which was something I hadn't felt in a while, job-wise, if ever.

"I think that's perfect for you, girl," Kori said later, after we placed our food truck taco order. I eat a lot, I realize. "You love all redecorating and design stuff."

"I do. I'm actually a little embarrassed that I didn't think of it myself."

"Doesn't even matter. You're thinking about it now."

"I've been checking out some schools. There are a couple I'm really interested in."

"How are you gonna pay for it, though? Aren't things already tight for you since Jada moved out?"

"Two words: tuition reimbursement. It's a hundred percent covered. BryCom is good for something."

"Damn, I didn't know they offered that! I could've milked them for some free education before I left there."

"You already have a master's degree, Kori."

"What, a chick can't go for a doctorate?"

Laughing, I leaned back in the plastic chair and kicked out my legs, feeling refreshingly optimistic. My money might have still been funny but at least I was happy. No more Jada drama, I was looking to start a new career path, my BFF's business was doing well, in love with my Cammy Bae. Maybe I needed to play the lottery, too.

I heard laughter over my shoulder and casually glanced back to try to see what was so funny, and I happened to see Cam a ways down the street. Sitting up straighter, I turned around.

"What's wrong?" Kori asked.

"Does that look like Cam or am I trippin'?" I asked, trying to avoid pointing by jerking my head in that direction.

Kori quickly stood, not trying to be discreet at all.

"Kori!" I hissed, frantically waving for her to sit down.

"What? Girl, he's way over there, and he's not even looking this way. Yeah, that looks like him. Why?"

"I...just didn't know he was gonna be over here..."

"What, did he tell you he was gonna be somewhere else or something? You think he's creepin'?"

"No! No, nothing like that. He comes over this way a lot. I guess I just...wasn't expecting to see him, that's all."

Kori sunk back into her chair, looking at me strangely. She clearly didn't see the big deal. "Okay..."

I looked over my shoulder again at Cam, who was just standing near the store he liked to buy his screen t-shirts from, sipping from a Starbucks cup while he scrolled through his phone. My eyes widened slightly when I saw a couple of women leave the shoe store next door. Both beautiful and totally Cam's type. And as loudly as they were talking, surely they'd catch his attention.

"Girl, what are you doing?" Kori asked from behind me. "Our order is up."

"Can you grab that?" My eyes were still on Cam. I watched as the women passed by him, one giving him a noticeably appreciative look as she put some more sway in her hips. Cam looked up at them, nodding politely before looking back at his phone. The women continued on down the street, and Cam did give them another glance that if I *chose* to read too much into it, could've been described as yearning.

"Nyla, you know this is sad, right?"

I turned to see Kori's knowing glare. "What? What do you mean?"

"Spying on your man already?"

"That's not...okay, it's not like I followed him. I didn't know he was going to be out here. All I was doing was just..."

"Checking to see if he looked at other women?"

"Okay? Is that so terrible?"

"And what would you have done if he had?"

"I...I don't know..."

"Nyla, you look at other men. You were just talking about how fine the crossing guard was."

"So? It's not like I was gonna do anything with him. I'm in a relationship with who I want."

"So why is it so hard to believe that Cam is, too?"

Knockout punch.

Kori opened up one of her tacos, putting extra green chile sauce on it before taking a huge bite. She had my tacos held hostage between her elbows on the table.

"Uh, you're just gonna eat that in my face? Can I have my food, please?"

"Not until you admit how stupid you're being right now."

"I didn't do anything, Kori."

"You're on some double standard bullshit and you low-key don't trust your man yet I'm willing to bet money I don't even have that he didn't do anything wrong."

"No, he didn't. I don't even know why I did that." I sighed, resting my chin in my hand. "I guess old habits die hard."

"As long as you know. You can have your tacos now." She slid them across the table.

"I hate you sometimes."

"Girl, if you're having doubts or concerns in your relationship, you need to let Cam know instead of trying to see what you can catch him in."

"I wasn't...okay, yeah, you're right. This is all in my own head; it's nothing he did."

"Okay. You get your hot sauce back for that." She pushed the packets towards me.

I just shook my head.

"Y'all are still good, right?"

"Yeah, we're great. I'm supposed to be seeing him later."

"Good. And I know you wanna look back over there so go ahead."

I whirled around in my seat, but Cam was walking away in the opposite direction towards his car. Once he was out of sight, my phone chimed with a text from him, saying he couldn't wait to see me later. My cheeks burned as I looked up at Kori sheepishly.

"Uh-huh," she smirked knowingly, munching on her taco.

It didn't matter that she didn't see the text. She knew I knew I was being silly.

I really needed to get it together because this paranoid stuff was for the birds.

After returning Cam's text, letting him know I couldn't wait to see him, either, I just unwrapped my tacos and tried to put the whole scene out of my mind.

I was sitting on some metal bleachers, trying to ignore the slight nip in the air while I watched Cam play pickup basketball with some of his friends. I could really take or leave basketball, but since I always whined about going with him to the games he had to cover for work, this was a compromise. And not a bad one, since watching my man sweaty and dunking and blocking shots was a turn-on I didn't expect but was surely enjoying. It wasn't long at all before me rubbing my legs together stopped being about the temperature outside.

"You're Nyla, yes?"

I looked to my left to see a man standing near me, his foot resting on the bottom bleacher. He looked vaguely familiar but I couldn't quite place him.

"Yeah."

"I figured. As much as he keeps looking over here at you after every other play."

I grinned, unable to help it. "Well, you know. And you are?"

"Glenn." He held a hand out, which I shook politely. "I was Cam's roommate in college."

"That's right!" I exclaimed, finally remembering. "I've seen a few pictures of y'all from back in the day. You had some really...*thick* cornrows."

He chuckled. "Yeah, you can say they were hideous. Everybody else sure did."

"I don't know you like that," I said with a grin.

"Well, I certainly feel like I know *you*. Cam talks about you incessantly." He nodded towards the bleachers. "May I?"

"Oh yeah, sure."

He took a seat on the bleacher rung just below mine. "I don't think I've seen you out here before."

"Yeah, I admit I'm not huge on sports. I like them okay but not nearly as much as Cam. But he sweet-talked me."

"No wonder he's out there showing off. I thought he had taken a Red Bull or something."

"He hates those," I replied, unable to resist the flaming in my cheeks. It warmed me to think that Cam was trying to put on a show just because I was out there watching. "You mean he doesn't go this hard every time he plays?"

"Not nearly. You saw those push-ups he did after he caught that alley-oop? Purely for your benefit."

I laughed. "Well, I'm not complaining about it."

Cam was watching us from the court, and his teammates had to remind him to get back in the game. I winked at him.

"It's good to see my friend so enamored," Glenn commented, seeing the exchange. "In the years I've known him,

I've never seen him so taken with anyone. And he's had his share of women."

He didn't have to add that part. "It's definitely mutual. Cam is..." I shook my head, trying to find the words. "He's just everything."

Glenn smiled. "I love to see it. Ever since I got back from Jamaica last year, he's been happier than I've ever seen him. Even when you two were just friends, he'd talk about you more than whoever he was dating."

This man was sending my ego through the roof. "Yeah? I didn't know that but I love hearing it. Is Jamaica where you're from? I hear the accent."

"Yes, I left there in my teens but I go back every few months, since my family remains there."

"Cam's told me about some of the trouble you two used to get into back in the day."

"Thankfully we've both matured," he replied, actually looking like he was blushing. His toasty brown skin was a little flushed. "I'm married with a baby on the way and he's head over heels for you."

I glanced at him. "Did Cam tell you to come over here and say all this?"

Confusion flashed across his face. "Not at all. He wouldn't have me do such a thing."

Immediately feeling silly, I tried to play it off by laughing. "Don't mind me. I think I'm just hungry, plus it's starting to get kinda windy out here. I don't know how they can play in this with no sleeves."

"It's not so bad when you're out there moving around a lot."

"How come you're not out there with them?"

"Bad knee."

"Ahh."

Glenn continued to keep me company while we watched the rest of Cam's games. I was ready to go, but that didn't mean I wasn't enjoying watching my man play or hear from his friend how much he talked about me when we were apart. I'd been around Cam's friends some since I'd known him but not a ton; part of me wondered what they thought about me, namely me and Cam together. Did they wonder why he chose me, of all people? They were cool to me but I had no way of knowing what they really thought.

Then I shook my head, snapping out of it. Who cared? Cam wanted to be with me, and that was all that mattered. If his friends said something negative about our relationship, that was for Cam to handle, and I'm sure he would've.

When it was *finally* time to leave, Glenn said goodbye before going on his way, and Cam came over to me, giving me a sweaty kiss.

"You see me out there, babe?"

"I sure did. You looked good, Cammy Bae."

"You might just be my good luck charm 'cause we won every game," he informed, slipping his hoodie over his head. "I'm gonna have to bring you out here more often."

"Oh..." I froze, causing him to laugh. "Uhh..."

"I'm kidding, Nyla."

"Oh, thank *god*."

"Though it *would* be nice if you came out every now and then."

"I must admit, you looked damn yummy out there, jumping all high and doing all those dunks and stuff. How 'bout I come out here for every time you go with me to the flea market."

"Damn you. But I'll take that compliment."

I laughed as he finished changing shoes (because apparently it's a sin to wear your basketball shoes for anything other than playing basketball) before taking my hand and leading me towards the gate of the fence surrounding the court. He stopped a couple of times to bump fists with some of his friends, and they all said good-bye to me, too, as everyone headed for their vehicles.

"You still coming back to my place, right?" he confirmed once we were in his car.

"Yep. I still have some clothes over there I can change into tomorrow."

"Good."

"We might need to go by the store, though, so I can get some body wash and a couple other toiletries. I forgot to bring mine and I'm not really trying to smell Mountain Man Fresh or whatever that stuff is you have."

He laughed, pausing in putting his seatbelt on. "Don't worry about it; I've got you."

"What do you mean?"

"You'll see."

Once we got back to his house, he led me to his bathroom, and I gasped once he turned on the light. There was a huge basket full of my favorite body washes, bath sponges, oils and body creams, toothpaste, mouthwash, and extra toothbrushes. There was even some sweet-scented shaving cream and razors. I guess he didn't love when I used his that time I needed a quick underarm shave.

"Cammy Bae," I gushed, grinning as I placed both hands on my chest. "This is so sweet of you!"

"I hope I remembered everything," he commented, sliding an arm around my shoulders. "I just didn't want you to have to worry about bringing a bunch of stuff when you came over here."

"Thank you *so* much." I hugged him around the waist, smiling wider when his arms encircled me and squeezed. "I might just have to go to all of your pickup games now."

He laughed. "Not why I did this but I'll take it. You hungry? 'Cause I am."

"I could eat."

"Lemme take a shower real quick then we'll grab something."

After stealing a couple of kisses, I stepped out of the bathroom so he could do his thing. Once I heard the shower water running, I toyed with the idea of joining him in there, but I hadn't reached that level of boldness yet.

By the time Cam emerged wearing nothing but sweatpants (*yes*) I had made some roast beef sandwiches with grilled onions, spinach, and tomatoes, and some tater tots that he had in the freezer. Cam had a tendency to take long showers so I had plenty of time.

"Thanks for this, baby," he said, taking a huge bite of his sandwich. "I didn't even realize just how hungry I was."

"I figured you would be, after playing all that ball. That's why I made you two sandwiches and gave you most of the tots."

"You fried these? I didn't think I had any oil..."

"You forgot you have an air fryer?"

"I actually did," he chuckled. He popped a tater tot into his mouth. "I stuck it under the cabinet and forgot about it."

"Shows how much you appreciate the gifts I give you. I use the heck out of mine."

"Oh, I know. I didn't even think you could air fry donuts. And it's not that I don't appreciate you getting me that; just haven't been doing a whole lot of cooking lately. You and work have been taking most of my energy."

"All is forgiven, then," I said with a smile.

We finished eating and Cam quickly cleaned the kitchen, refusing to let me help since I made our lunch. As I watched him wipe down the counters, noting the muscles of his bare back and how his ass looked in those sweatpants, I felt my arousal click on. It was amazing how Cam affected me like that; even watching him clean the kitchen got me hot.

"You know," I ventured, moving over to him and sliding my hands up his back. "I wasn't kidding earlier when I said you looked yummy out there today."

"Yeah?" He glanced at me over his shoulder, smirking and showing that dimple.

"Absolutely." My hands slid down to his butt, then to his hard thighs. "And I especially enjoyed learning that you like to talk about me when you're around your boys."

"I guess I shouldn't be surprised Glenn told you about that. He likes to talk a lot."

"You didn't want me to know?"

"It's not that." He turned to face me, rubbing his hands up and down my arms. "I didn't even realize how much I talked about you around them until one of them told me to either do something about it or shut the hell up."

I giggled, though my hands were still feeling him up.

"Glenn was actually the one who pointed out to me first that I clearly had feelings for you that were deeper than I thought," Cam continued. "I never went on and on about anybody like I did about you, not even back in the day. And every time I started dating somebody else, Glenn predicted it wouldn't last because I really wanted you...but I was running from it."

My eyes roamed his face. "You agree with that?"

"It makes sense."

"Why would you do that?"

"I guess...I don't know. The day we met, when I was behind you in line at Starbucks, I was attracted to you then. And I've never been shy about approaching women but for whatever reason, I didn't know what to say to you to break the ice. I'd never experienced that, ever. Then when the thing happened outside with the guy that was gonna jump you, I didn't hesitate to step in. It's wild to say that I'm actually glad that happened because it got me close to you."

"Wow..."

"Then we hit it off so well right off the bat; I've never had a connection with anybody like I have with you, Nyla." He pulled me closer, looking at me lovingly. "But I'll admit that it freaked me out. And I wasn't sure if you looked at me like that or what you'd think if I confessed what I felt to you; guess I thought you'd think I was scheming or something. And I didn't want to do anything to mess up what we had. So I just took on the protective, big brother-type role, even though that's not how I looked at you at *all*."

"You did an excellent job of hiding that. Because I never once saw you look at me any other way. Until I wore those booty shorts, that is."

"Yeah, I had no defense against those." We shared a laugh. "But believe me, when we weren't around each other, you were on my mind a *lot*. I tried to convince myself that we were better off as just friends, though that's not what I really wanted. That's why I let myself get distracted by other women; I thought – hoped – that one of them would pull me out of the feelings I had for you that I was running from. But," his grip on my waist tightened. "None of them could."

"Cam," I whispered, floored by this new information. "So all the time I was pining and yearning for you..."

"I was doing the same for you."

"And you sexing Jada where you knew I could hear you...what was that?"

"I was on some bullshit with that, and I know it," he admitted, looking away shamefully. "That was more of me doing the most to try to distract myself from going for you like I wanted to. But it was fucked up and I know if the roles were reversed, it would have sent me through the roof to hear you with another man. I already almost lost it when I saw you kissing on Kendrick that time."

"I recall. 'Cause you surely lost it when I told you I slept with him."

"I know. That drove me crazy."

"Just like it drove *me* crazy every time I saw or heard you with Jada. Or anybody else."

"I get it. Really, in my head, you've always been mine, Nyla." His hand gripped the back of my neck. "Even when I was running from it, being stupid, fighting it...it was you that I wanted. And now that I have you, I'm good. I don't want this to change any time soon."

"Me either, Cam. And part of me wants to be mad at you for waiting so long to tell me all this..."

"Like you didn't do the same thing?"

"Don't be pointing out facts."

"We were *both* some punks," he concluded, playfully tweaking my chin. "I just hate to think about all the time we wasted."

"Well, let's not waste any more." I leaned up for a kiss, which he quickly obliged. As the kiss deepened, I slipped my hand under the waistband of his pants, glad that he wasn't wearing any underwear. I began stroking him, causing him to moan against my lips.

"Baby..." he whispered, biting his lip as his eyes slid closed and his head fell back.

I wordlessly sank to my knees, pulling his pants down as I went. After stroking him a few more times with my hands, I slid my mouth over his hardness, loving the hiss I heard from above me when I did.

"Shit, Nyla..." His voice had that gruff sex edge that I loved, and it just made me go harder. One of his hands gripped the edge of the counter while the other grabbed a handful of my hair, his hips smoothly matching my rhythm. "Fuck!"

I teased the inside of his thighs with my tongue, causing him to shudder, hard. "You wanna take this to the bedroom?"

"I wanna take you right here," he muttered, reaching down and snatching me up. He hurriedly yanked my pants and underwear down before hoisting me onto the counter, stepping out of his sweatpants and kicking them across the floor. I opened my legs wide for him, as ready and eager as he was.

"Should I get a condom?" he panted, the head of his dick right at my opening. He kissed my lips, then my neck. "I will if you want me to."

"No, just fuck me," I ordered breathlessly, gripping him tighter. We had talked about going without condoms and had both recently been tested, but just hadn't gone there yet. But I surely wanted to go there now. I was literally aching for it. "*Now*, Cam, please..."

He wasted no time sliding inside me, and the air in Cam's kitchen was quickly filled with plenty of cussin' from both of us about how good it felt. He grabbed hold of my hips and let me have it, and I welcomed every hard stoke he gave. Sex with Cam was like a drug, and I was a proud junkie. No issues with the fantasy-matching there.

We were just finishing and about to head to his bedroom for round two when there was a knock on the door. Cam cursed under his breath.

"Who is it?" he barked towards the door, his frustration evident.

There was a pause. "It's Jada."

Chapter 16

Cam and I looked at each other, both of us jarred.

"What is *she* doing here?" I hissed.

"No idea. I haven't even talked to her since we broke up."

"You gonna let her in?"

More knocks on the door. "Cam," Jada called out. "Open the door."

Cam didn't budge. "I'm busy, Jada."

"I just need five minutes."

"I don't have five minutes."

"*Two* minutes."

"He doesn't have that, either," I called out before Cam could respond. Cam glanced at me with an amused look. Oh well. I wasn't sure if he was gonna let her know I was there so I did it myself.

"Nyla?" Jada's voice sounded surprised. "What are *you* doing over here?"

"I'm almost *sure* you don't really wanna know that."

"What does *that* mean? Cam??"

Sighing, Cam looked at me, silently asking my permission to let her in. I just returned his look, unbothered. She could sit out there all day, for all I cared.

"Cam!" Jada practically yelled, banging on the door now.

"Okay, she's getting on my damn nerves," I muttered.

"Damn it!" Cam exclaimed, yanking his sweatpants back on.

"Hmph," I scoffed, not happy that he seemed to be relenting. I took my time getting my jeans and shirt.

Cam eyed me, sensing my attitude. "I don't want her in here any more than you do, baby, but I'm tired of her banging on my door."

"I'd just call the police, if it were me. Don't you have some sprinklers you can turn on?"

"Nyla."

"Whatever, Cam. Just let her in, if that's what you wanna do. But I'm timing it."

"You and me both."

Once I was decent, he stalked over to the door and yanked it open, finally putting an end to the constant knocking. Jada stood there in a body-hugging orange mini dress and heels, her seductive expression already in place. Her round pouty lips were adorned with a shiny glittery (tacky) lipstick. She was noticeably jarred when Cam's deep scowl didn't move.

"What do you want?" he asked her.

Jada's eyes flitted to me, then back to Cam. I could tell she was trying to keep up the flirtatious vibe. "Can I come in?"

"Not until you tell me what you're doing here."

"I need to talk to you."

"That's what phones are for, Jada."

"We both know you wouldn't have answered if I called you. Come on, Cam, please?"

Cam glanced back at me before stepping back. Jada grinned as she entered, eying me as if she expected me to automatically retreat. Cam closed the door behind her and moved over to stand next to me, both of us looking at her expectantly.

"Um, Nyla, would you mind giving us a minute?" Jada asked me.

"Yeah."

"Great, thanks." Then it must have registered what I actually said. "Wait, what?"

"I *would* mind. So just get on with it 'cause Cam and I were busy." I glanced at my watch. "Two minutes goes fast, so start talking."

Jada's jaw dropped slightly as she looked at Cam, but he just put an arm around my shoulder and waited.

"Wait a minute..." Jada said, catching on. "Are you two *together*??"

"We're the definition of it," Cam confirmed. "Now I ask again; what do you want?"

"I thought you always said you two were just friends!" Jada looked at us accusingly. "I *knew* something was going on with y'all! Here I am, coming back over here to see if we can work things out and I find out you were cheating on me!"

"First off, nobody cheated on you. Nyla and I got together *after* you and I split. Secondly, and most importantly, there is no working things out so if that's all you're here for, you're straight wasting your time."

"*And* that thirst-trap dress," I added. "Though it *is* cute, I admit."

Jada looked back and forth between me and Cam as if she was trying to decide if we were just messing with her or not.

"Why are you over here, anyway? Didn't you go back to your ex?" I asked her, unable to resist.

"That...that was a mistake. He's smothering me. Just because I slipped up once when we were together the first time, he feels like he has to know where I am every hour of the damn day. I can't live like that."

"Oh well," Cam shrugged. "Not my problem."

"Why are you acting like this?" Jada stepped closer, eyes on Cam. She really had a lot of nerve, doing this right in my face. "You *know* we had something good, Cam. There's no way you're over me just like that."

I tensed up, and Cam reassuringly squeezed my shoulder before stepping behind me and sliding his arms around my waist. He leaned down and nuzzled my neck, taking his time and actually licking me, causing me to giggle a little bit. It tickled some but mostly, I was giddy that he was taunting her like he was.

He finally lifted his head and looked at Jada, pulling me even closer. She was standing there steaming, like she was about to explode.

"Like I said, you're wasting your time," Cam told her. He gently nudged me with his crotch. "Time check, baby."

"Thirty seconds left," I informed, not even looking at my watch.

Jada scoffed, her frown deepening. "So you're really trying to tell me you'd prefer *her* over *me*?? Are you serious?? Cam, there's no way-"

"Jada, when you *slipped up* on your ex, was it with the same guy that dropped you off *that* night or somebody else?" I interrupted. "You remember? When we both got home after midnight and you begged me not to tell Cam about it, swearing up and down that he was just a friend? Or did you decide to tell Cam about that already?"

It was funny how I could actually see the color drain from Jada's face.

"First I'm hearing about that," Cam spoke up, a slight edge in his voice. Was he upset?

"Cam, you...you *see* what she's trying to do!" Jada stammered, pointing a long manicured nail at me. "Don't listen to her. That guy was just-"

"Don't care. And your time is up." Cam released me and went over to the door, averting Jada's attempt to grab his arm as he passed. He opened the door and looked her square in the eye. "Do not call me. Quit tagging me in your thirty social media posts. And if you show up at my door again, I'm calling the cops. We're *done*."

Jada looked thoroughly embarrassed. I'm sure she had no doubt that showing up in that barely-there dress and her sex kitten heels and her stupid-looking lipstick would be all it took to get Cam swooning over her again. Getting her face cracked like this surely never entered her mind, especially the part about Cam choosing me over her. She wouldn't have believed that in a million years.

Shooting me a final glare, she finally stomped towards the door, and was barely over the threshold when Cam slammed it behind her, locking it.

"You okay?" I asked after a few moments of him just standing there looking at the floor, stewing.

"I'm fine." He looked at me. "Though what is this about you catching her coming home in some guy's car? You never told me about that."

"It wasn't my business to tell, Cam. I kept telling y'all I didn't want to be involved in your relationship. Please don't tell me you're actually upset about that."

"No, no, I'm not," he quickly replied, moving over to me.

"You're asking me about it."

"'Cause it was new information. If this was a couple months ago, yeah, I'd be pissed. But now, moot point. I just find it curious that you kept it to yourself, that's all."

I cocked my head to the side. "And...why is that?"

"Because if you were dating somebody and you found out they were out with some other woman, and I knew about it and didn't tell you, you'd feel some kind of way about it. Would probably cuss me out 'til my ears were sore then not talk to me for a month."

Okay, he had a point. I wouldn't have been okay with finding out about Cam keeping that kind of information from me, and I knew it. As my friend, my *best* friend, I would have expected him to let me know about it immediately, regardless.

"You're right," I admitted. "Even if it doesn't matter now, I'm sorry about that. I should've told you. At the time, I told myself I didn't care what happened with you two. But of course that was my extreme jealousy clouding my good judgment."

He chuckled, taking my face in his hands. Leaning down, he brushed his lips against mine. "I get it. And I appreciate the apology."

"Show me by giving me a *real* kiss, then."

Grinning, he gathered me in his arms and laid one on me, stroking that tongue against mine just the way I loved it. Keeping the kiss going, I grabbed the sides of his waist and started walking backwards towards his bedroom so he could get back to stroking something else.

"I must say, Kori, I'm not used to seeing you so nervous. You're usually the one that calms *me* down about stuff."

"Well, I can't help it. I need this to go well."

"It will."

"Nyla, this is my first event where I've actually invited the press to Sleek. More importantly, *Chrisette Clarke* is gonna be here. It'll be the first time she's been by since the opening."

"Why are you worried, though? I thought you said everything was going well. You were even able to finally hire someone to handle your social media stuff and things picked up, right?"

"Yeah, and that's great, but I'm just nervous about Chrisette being here *watching* me sell her stuff."

"You don't have anything to worry about. You've done a lot of promotion for this, most of the people you invited RSVP'd, the boutique looks great, and you look even better. Just chill and do your thing; it's going to be amazing."

Taking a deep breath, she ran her hands over her fresh braids and closed her eyes, calming herself. She did a long exhale and shook her hands out, rocking her head from side to side and bouncing on her toes, like I imagine she probably did before all of her basketball games back in the day.

"Thanks for that, girl," she finally said, shooting me a grateful smile. "I appreciate the proverbial shot in the arm."

"Anytime."

Things kicked off not too long after that and thankfully Kori had managed to shake off her nerves and be her usual charming self, working the room. I saw her newly-hired social media manager taking pictures and filming, getting shots of Kori with the press, customers happily holding up their bags full of purchases, and people milling around conversing. There were light refreshments over in the corner, which was my job for the day; I was to keep everything stocked and make sure no one took drinks to the sales floor. Lord knew Kori would freak out if any of Chrisette Clarke's designs got red punch on them.

Speaking of Chrisette Clarke, she and her husband Dorian arrived about a half hour into the event, and I saw Kori's face light up. She immediately went over to them, greeting both with warm hugs. She and Chrisette immediately launched into an excited hushed chat before Kori led her over to some people for introductions. I grinned, thrilled that things were going so well for my friend.

Not too long after that, Cam came in. He looked around for a moment before spotting me, smiling and immediately snaking through the crowd to get to me.

"Welcome to Sleek," I playfully greeted him.

"Kori's got you on cookie duty, huh?" he chuckled, giving me a peck on the lips.

"Yep. Elsa has to run the register and Kori is schmoozing everyone. I don't mind, though. I'm just glad it's going so well 'cause she was super nervous about all this."

"There sure are a lot of people. If most of them actually buy stuff, she's gonna rack up today."

"That's the plan. So you need to find something in here you like."

"I'll definitely get something. Glenn said he was going to come by with his wife, too."

"Oh, that's great!"

Cam kept me company as things continued, only leaving my side when Glenn and his wife arrived. I also recognized a couple of the other guys Cam played ball with come in with their ladies, and it made my heart surge to know that Cam had invited them there to help Kori.

Eventually, Kori made her way over to us. She gave Cam a brief hug and thanked him for coming before grabbing my hand.

"You mind if I steal our girl for a minute, Cam? I want to introduce her to someone."

"As long as it's not another dude, go ahead," Cam joked, though I'm sure he meant that.

"Technically it is, but it's totally professional," Kori insisted. "And I think we all know there's not a man in here that could take Nyla's attention from you. She is irreversibly sprung and in love."

"That's what I wanna hear," Cam replied with a smile, winking at me. "Go on and do your thing. I'll man things over here."

"Thanks, Cammy Bae," I grinned as Kori pulled me away.

He just shook his head, chuckling.

"Cammy Bae, really?" Kori teased, glancing down at me. "You couldn't come up with anything better than that?"

"Hush."

"Anyway," Kori said as we approached a dark chocolate hunk of man that would've definitely made me weak in the knees if I wasn't already so Cam-high. "I wanted to introduce you to the Furniture God, Dorian Clarke. Dorian, this is my best friend and *huge* fan of yours, Nyla Nelson."

Dorian smiled and shook his head at Kori before turning his dark eyes to me, removing his hand from his pocket and holding it out to me. "A pleasure to meet you, Nyla. And please tell your friend to quit calling me that."

"I'll do no such thing, Mr. Clarke. Your pieces are amazing. It blows my mind that you make all of those things with your bare hands."

He placed a hand to his chest and bowed his head gratefully. "I appreciate that. It's just what I love to do. And chill with that Mr. Clarke stuff; I'm just Dorian."

"Well, Dorian, I'm sure Kori has probably blabbed by now about how much I've been raving over your work. There are more than a few on my wish list."

"That's really flattering," he said with a smile, briefly ducking his head. Was he blushing? It only made me even more of a fan. "Maybe we can work something out, then. I definitely want my furniture with people that will appreciate it."

"Oh, I'd love that, but you do custom pieces for celebrities and dignitaries and politicians-"

"All just people; no more special than anybody else," Dorian waved off my comment. "Only thing those titles mean is that I can charge them more."

I grinned. I was officially his groupie. (A respectful one, though).

"Another thing I *blabbed* to him about was your interior design skills," Kori chimed in, looking at me pointedly. "I'm sure he's probably tired of hearing about you by now."

"Yeah, she's been hyping you up pretty hard," Dorian chuckled. "And she showed me pictures of what you did to her spot, and told me you even helped out designing this store. You've got some skills, girl."

My face flaming, I was momentarily stumped. "Oh wow, thanks so much!"

"Chrisette and I have been discussing a few things and I'd like to talk to you about some business opportunities. I need someone to stage a few properties we have, plus the designer we hired for our bed and breakfast had to back out because of a death in the family. Would you be interested-"

"*Hell* yeah!" I exclaimed, then immediately put a hand over my mouth. My eager ass. But Dorian just laughed.

"Hey, I like that," he assured me good naturedly, the smile still on his face. "I *love* that enthusiasm. I did the same thing the first time somebody wanted to buy one of my pieces. Don't be embarrassed at all."

"I'm just..." My hand dropped to my chest, still floored. "*So* flattered that you're even considering me."

"Folks gave me a shot when I started out, so I definitely do the same. Chrisette loves interior design, too, but she has her hands full with the kids and her clothing lines already; neither of us want her to take on anything else right now. So you'd actually be helping us as much as we'd be helping you."

"I'd absolutely, absolutely love to work with you two on this and whatever else, Mr. Clarke...I mean, Dorian." I tried to calm myself down, though my heart was beating a mile a second. "In the interest of full disclosure, though, I don't have any formal training or even a large portfolio to show you. I *did* re-do my man's place and a neighbor of mine's living room; I can show you pictures of those, as well as the changes I made to my own apartment..."

Dorian didn't flinch. "I'm not sweating any of that, as far as the training and portfolio stuff. Everybody has to start somewhere. I started making furniture in my high school workshop; that's as far as my 'formal training' went. I had a natural gift and a love for it, and just kept working on my craft. That's all that matters, in my opinion. School is fine but there's nothing like hands-on experience. And you'll learn more as you go, like I did. So I'll be glad to see your pictures but it'll just cement what I already know. Believe me, Nyla, Chrisette and I have been doing this long enough to know what we like."

I owed Kori *big-time* for this.

We all talked for a few more minutes before Dorian and Kori introduced me to Chrisette, who was just as much of a sweetheart as Kori always said she was. Dorian gave me his card and told me to call his assistant to set up a time to meet before he and Chrisette went around to say their goodbyes, as they had to leave for another event and then pick up their kids. I was admittedly in awe as I watched them leave hand-in-hand, the picture of down-to-earth Black excellence, and I just knew things were only going to get better for me from then on out. I could feel it with everything in me, and I became overcome with an optimism that I'd literally never felt in regards to my future.

I walked back over to Cam on shaky legs, still clutching Dorian's card and marveling over the last twenty minutes.

"You okay?" Cam asked, concerned. He gently grabbed my arm as I got close to him.

"Cam...I'm *great*," I assured him, the grin spreading across my face like a happy rash. "I'm amazing!"

"What happened?" he asked, smiling cautiously.

"I'll...I'll tell you all about it when we leave here. I'm still processing that it happened at all. But we *definitely* need to celebrate tonight!"

"Yeah? Whatever it is, I'm glad to see you so happy. And I mean, *really* happy," he chuckled as I actually started jumping up and down a little bit. I couldn't help it; I was over the moon excited!

Thankfully, it wasn't too much longer before things started winding down. I was itching to get out of there and gush to Cam about my new opportunity; I didn't want to get into it in a room full of people.

There was the ever-present teeny tiny nervous part of me that expected Dorian or Chrisette to come back in saying they changed their minds, but the larger part of me knew better. Neither of them seemed like the type to bullshit anyone, and from what I'd read about Dorian, he was a former delinquent from the rough part of town who turned his life around, meeting and falling hard for Chrisette, who was from money but never acted like it or treated him like he was beneath her. People saying he was nothing but a hood that wouldn't amount to anything fueled him. Everything he had, he earned, and he was quick to give credit to everyone who helped him along the way. I couldn't imagine someone who had been through all of that yanking my chain for the hell of it.

Cam and I stayed and helped Kori get the store cleaned up and waited for her and Elsa to close everything out, and then we finally left. Cam followed me to my place, and we were barely through the door before I was shrieking the news about my offer from Dorian, finally releasing my corked excitement.

"Whoa, are you serious??" Cam exclaimed as I jumped around my living room. I was sure the people who lived below me were probably cussing me out. He grinned and caught me in his arms, swinging me around. "That's amazing, baby!"

"I know! I'm still...I just can't believe it!" I rested my arms around his shoulders, looking at him dreamily. "Little ol' me, getting to work with Furniture God Dorian Clarke. My mind is *blown* right now."

"I still say that's a pretty ballsy nickname to have."

"That's what Kori and I call him. He's way too humble and down-to-earth to give himself that name."

"I didn't get to meet him or his wife but they did seem really nice, from the conversations I managed to overhear earlier," Cam noted, gently returning me to my feet.

"Oh my god...I should've introduced you!" I gasped, touching my fingertips to my lips and looking at him apologetically. "I'm *so* sorry!"

"Stop. I'm not sweating that. I'll meet them at some point, I'm sure. I'm just glad that they're giving you a chance to show your skills. You nervous about it?"

I paused, considering the question. "Surprisingly, not really," I realized. "I'm more anxious than anything; now that it's on the table, I just want to jump in and get started. I'm more worried about doing something to embarrass myself; you know I get extra clumsy when I'm really excited."

He laughed. "You're gonna knock it out of the park, baby; I already know. You have a gift for this. What about BryCom, though? What's this gonna mean for your job there?"

"I haven't even thought about all that, honestly. I'm just focusing on meeting with Dorian and Chrisette and getting the details of what they want me to do. I might be able to do both. I don't know. For the time being, I just want to enjoy this high I'm on right now. I have a great new opportunity, I'm in love with the man of my dreams..."

Grinning, Cam eyed my hands as they started unbuttoning his shirt. "You're gonna try to wear me out tonight, aren't you?"

"You take workout supplements and spend a bunch of time in the gym; you can handle it."

"Hey, wear me out, then." He bit his lip as I started tonguing his chest. "I'm all yours."

"You better be. Now get those damn pants off."

He followed my instruction as I lifted my dress over my head, tossing it aside. Once we were both naked, I threw a blanket over the couch before pushing him down onto it and straddling his lap, wasting no time joining us together. Cam clutched me to him with both arms, burying his face between my breasts as I rode him like a madwoman.

"*Damn*, Nyla," Cam panted as I pushed him down onto his back, looking up at me in mild surprise. "I've never seen you like this..."

"I've never *felt* like this," I quickly replied, bracing my hands on his chest and putting extra bounce in my hips. Emotion started to battle my arousal for front and center. "I'm *so* happy to be with you, Cam, you have no idea..."

"I bet I do, 'cause I'm just as happy to be with you, babe." He looked up at me as my hips slowed, the emotion winning the battle and tears starting to form in my eyes. We just looked at each other, our hands still languidly sliding along each other's bodies. Eventually Cam reached up and wiped my tears before bringing my face to his for a long, deep kiss.

We spent the rest of the night on the couch, touching and enjoying each other. Once Cam started to doze off, I laid my head on his chest and sighed, trying not to freak out about just how content I felt in that moment.

Then suddenly I sat up in realization, looking at Cam with a slight frown of concern mixed with worry.

Chapter 17

"Is the champagne really necessary? I would've been fine with a stack of tacos."

The smile remained on my face as I accepted the glass from Kori as she waved away my statement with her other hand.

"I know you love you some tacos but news like this deserves the good stuff."

"Well, I appreciate it. It *is* pretty amazing."

"It's more than that. You went up in Clarke Enterprises with all of four design jobs under your belt and blew them away. Those houses you staged for them were snatched up damn near as soon as they put them on the market."

"I don't know if I can take all the credit for that."

"You can take a lot of it. And Chrisette can't say enough about the job you're doing with their bed and breakfast. They didn't offer to make you their *in-house designer* for nothing!"

We both squealed and wiggled in our seats, equally as excited. Dorian and Chrisette were so impressed with my work that they made me an offer to come on board with them full-time, and of *course* I accepted; it was a no-brainer, especially when I saw how much they were going to pay me. I put in my two-week notice at BryCom the same damn day.

"Kori, I can't thank you enough for recommending me to them," I told her for what had to be the hundredth time. "This wouldn't even be happening if it weren't for you."

"Maybe not right now or exactly like this but it would've happened, eventually," Kori assured. "You were already about to start your journey to this. All I did was nudge you towards the express lane."

"And believe me, I'll never forget it. Or be able to repay you for it."

"Girl, please, as much as you helped me when I was opening my store; giving me all that encouragement when I was pussyfooting around it, keeping me from going crazy from getting all the paperwork and permits and all that shit, and stepping in however you could, even working the front counter when Elsa got sick? You don't owe me *anything*, trust me."

"I love you, girl," I gushed, reaching over for a hug.

"I love you, too."

A slight frown eased onto my face as I pulled away. I put my champagne flute on Kori's coffee table and rubbed my thighs anxiously.

"What's wrong?" she asked, noting my sudden change in demeanor.

"I'm...I'm kinda worried about something."

"With the new job?"

"No, not that. With Cam."

She frowned, putting her own glass down. "What's going on? You two have a fight?"

"No, we're good. For the most part."

"I'm confused, Nyla..."

"Please don't think that this is me being paranoid or looking for trouble, because I'm really not," I began. "But it occurred to me that since Cam and I became a couple, he hasn't told me he loves me."

Kori's eyebrows shot up. "For real?"

"He used to say it all the time when we were just friends; at least, often enough. But now that we're together romantically, nada. I know I've made comments about how in love with him I am and he didn't reciprocate it either time."

"And you think that means something?"

I looked at her. "Shouldn't I?"

"It's just hard for me to believe that his feelings for you have anything but deepened since you two hit 'bae' level. Especially after he confessed the stuff about carrying a torch for you from the beginning. I told you so, by the way."

"Hush."

"What did he say when you asked him about it?"

Pursing my lips, I looked away sheepishly.

"Nyla..."

"Okay, okay...I know what you're gonna say; that I should just ask him about it instead of sitting around over-analyzing. And you're right. I guess I just didn't want to seem silly or come across as insecure. After all we went through to get here, I don't want him to think I'm nitpicking about anything."

"Then just watch how you come at him about it but if you're curious or concerned, there's nothing wrong with asking," Kori informed me. "I'm sure it's nothing intentional; he probably doesn't even realize he's doing that, I bet."

I hunched a shoulder. "Maybe."

"Stop stressing yourself out and just ask the man," Kori ordered, picking up her flute and taking a long sip. "For the time being, though, let's drink this champagne and celebrate your new career."

I was supposed to meet Cam later, and Kori's advice rang in my head as I waited for him to come over. I knew he was covering a game and had to get his story submitted by the deadline that night, so I had some time.

While I waited, I busied myself with the redecorations I was planning for Jada's old room. I thought about just keeping it as a guest bedroom, but when did I have guests? It would be better suited as an office, where I could plan and keep swatches and samples and all those kinds of things. Dorian said I'd have an office over at Clarke Enterprises, but I also wanted a space to work at home, too. Kori thought I should get a bigger place since I was making significantly more money now, but I actually liked my little apartment, especially now that I had put my own spin on it and turned it into something I looked forward to coming home to. I was sure I'd outgrow it at some point but for the time being, I was good.

I was writing down some measurements for the window treatments when I heard Cam come in. Glancing at my watch, I stretched and headed out to the living room, surprised that so much time had passed already.

"Hey Cammy Bae," I greeted with a smile, padding over to him and reaching up for a hug.

He held me tightly before leaning back and planting a lingering kiss on my lips. "Hey, baby. I'm sorry I'm so late; the damn game went into overtime. I had to scramble to get the article submitted before midnight."

"It's fine; I figured it was something like that. Did you get to eat anything?"

"Just some pizza at the game. Is there any more beer in there?"

I looked at him curiously. "You really want a beer this late?"

"I've wanted one all night but I don't like to drink while I work. And it's been a long, frustrating day."

"Say no more." I went and grabbed a couple of beers from the fridge while Cam peeled off his jacket and kicked off his shoes. He dropped tiredly onto the couch, leaning his head back and closing his eyes.

I set the beers on the coffee table (on coasters) and sat down next to him, rubbing a hand along his thigh. "Why don't you go and get in the bed? You look exhausted."

"I'm all right; I'm tired but I'm not sleepy, really. Plus, I haven't seen you all day." He placed a hand over mine and smiled before sitting up and grabbing one of the beers, taking a long swig. "How was work?"

"It was awesome," I gushed, grinning automatically. "I am *so* amped about these new projects Dorian and Chrisette have coming up. And the bed and breakfast is coming along great. At first I was a little worried about taking on something of that size myself but between their encouragement and the people they have in place to help me, it's turning out to be a fun challenge. I actually have *assistants*, can you believe it?? I got to help hire my own design team!"

"That's wild. Look at you, running shit already."

I giggled. "We're gonna have to go back up there this weekend."

"When is the grand opening?"

"Two months. I'm like a kid counting down to Christmas."

"It's hard to believe you've been working with them ...what, it's been like six weeks or something by now, right?"

"Just about. And I know; this time had just flown by. I actually look forward to going to work. It actually doesn't even *feel* like work, I love it so much. I know I've given Kori a ton of credit and gratitude for hyping me up to Dorian but you certainly deserve your share, too."

His eyebrows rose in surprise as he took another swig of beer. "Me? What did I do?"

"You're the one that told me I needed to consider interior design as a career, remember? I was just over here thinking it was nothing more than a hobby to keep me sane while I worked my boring office job."

"I might've put the idea in your head but you're the one that had the skills to run with it. This is your calling. I'm damn proud of you, baby." He put his beer back on the coaster and pulled me closer to him, wrapping his arms around me and resting his forehead against mine. "I'm happy when you're happy."

"I'm amazingly happy," I whispered, playing with the collar of his shirt. I wondered if this was a good time to mention what was on my mind. "Cam, I..."

"Yeah?"

"There's something..." I looked up at him, noting the concerned look in those puppy dog eyes, and lost my nerve. "You know what, never mind. It's nothing."

"Uh-uh, don't do that," he retorted, stopping me from pulling away. "If there's something on your mind, tell me."

"I just...I don't want you to get the wrong idea."

"The wrong idea about what? What's going on, baby?"

"Cam, do you love me?" I finally blurted, scooting back a little so I could look fully at his face.

He blinked. "What kind of question is that? You *know* I love you."

"I know you love me as a *friend*. But you've never really said it in the romantic sense...you know, since we got together."

"What?"

"Are you in love with me, Cam? If you're not, it's okay...either you are or you're not, and it's certainly not something I want to try to pressure or guilt you into. I just want to know, for myself."

He looked at me for a long moment before sitting up and turning his body towards mine. He took my hands in his, gripping them tightly.

"I am absolutely, one hundred percent, undoubtedly, unflinchingly, irreversibly in love with you, Ms. Nelson." His voice was strong and his eyes stayed locked on mine, making sure to get the point across. "And it's not anything new. If I haven't made that known to you, that's my bad; I don't ever want you to doubt how I feel about you, baby."

"You show me in how you treat me every day, and please know I recognize and appreciate that," I quickly assured. "I guess I just...you've always been so expressive with the L-word before, it made me wonder if something had changed-"

"The only thing that's changed," he interrupted, placing a gentle finger to my lips, "Is the *amount* of love I have. The desire I have for you. The pride I have in being your man while still being your best friend. The thoughts about our future together. All of that has multiplied by the day since we made this thing official. And you won't ever have to wonder about it again." His voice broke a little, and he swallowed, his eyes shining with sincerity. "I promise you that. I love you *so* much, Nyla."

I threw my arms around his neck as the emotion from his words smacked me full force. I'm not sure what I had expected him to say, but what he *did* say literally sent chills up my spine and warmed me all over at the same time. His words were already replaying through my mind, and the more they did, the tighter I held onto Cam. I couldn't get close enough.

He pulled me onto his lap, holding me just as tightly. I just cried into this shoulder, smiling the whole time, while he kissed my neck and whispered how it was me and him, for as long as we both wanted it to be.

I don't know how much time passed before we slowly pulled apart, taking each other's faces in our hands.

"Are we good?" he asked me, kissing my forehead before going for my lips.

Nodding, I eagerly returned his kiss, smiling through all the tears. "We're better than good. And I love you, too."

However this had become my life, I wasn't going to question it. I was just going to thank God every day and make damn sure I didn't mess it up.

THE END

I surely hope you enjoyed Nyla and Cam's story (I definitely had fun writing it lol). Thank you so much for reading!

And did you recognize the cameos from *When You Share Too Much*? No? Probably should go ahead and read that one, too, then. *wink wink* lol

If you enjoyed this, please consider leaving a review. They're invaluable. And if you want to show *extra* love, share that you read *Forehead Kiss* on social media! ☺

You can find me on Instagram, Threads, FB, and TikTok at @authorjessicaterry. And don't forget to subscribe to my email list at jessicaterry.com.

Also by Jessica Terry

Some Like 'em Thick
It's All Right...Now
Not By a Long Shot
Get Right
Decisions and Consequences
Take One For the Team
When You Share Too Much
Backtalk
Emasculated
Restless
The Beginning of Again
Always and Nevers
She is Me
Split By the Bell
The Karma Call
Forehead Kiss
All Because of Ava
Love Intolerant
Mr. Time Waster
The Stubborn Kind
From Meltdown to Mistletoe
Mrs. Soul Crusher
I Want Us
Trade Rumors

Sugar Daddy Sweet Tooth
More Than What It Is
Hooked on Valentine's
Forced
Holliday Drama
Couple's Night
Liz and Luther
Chillin' on Thanksgiving
The Hired Gift
<u>The Introvert Series</u>
An Introvert's Christmas
Wooing the Introvert
The Introvert Roast
I, Take Thee Introvert
The Introvert Series Compilation (paperback only)

Discussion Questions

1. Nyla claimed to have been in love with Cam since the day they met. Do you think the way he came to her rescue had anything to do with her fast feelings?

2. There were many times throughout the story where Nyla chickened out about telling Cam how she felt about him. Would you have had the same trouble telling a friend you had romantic feelings for them?

3. Cam got hot and heavy with Nyla's roommate Jada pretty fast. Do you think this was inconsiderate of him or did he not do anything wrong?

4. Speaking of Jada, what did you think of her? Do you believe she was sincerely into Cam or was she just out to have fun?

5. Nyla had a tendency to be skittish when it came time to make changes, despite them being changes she said she wanted. Is this understandable or was she just being a coward?

6. Was Kori being too hard on Nyla about coming clean about her feelings for Cam? Was she insensitive to how hard it was or was she giving Nyla the pushes she needed?

7. Cam revealed that he had romantic feelings for Nyla initially, also, but chose to keep things at friendship, opting to play the protective role. Do you think this

was cowardly or commendable?

8. Cam got jealous of Kendrick or any man that showed interest in Nyla. Did he go overboard with his protectiveness of her?

9. Nyla was basically settling in her career. Did it surprise you that other people had to point out interior design as an option, given her obvious love for it?

10. Do you feel Nyla was too paranoid? Did she make things harder for herself or were her fears and issues justified? Did you find her frustrating?

Don't miss out!

Visit the website below and you can sign up to receive emails whenever Jessica Terry publishes a new book. There's no charge and no obligation.

https://books2read.com/r/B-A-NVYK-LVTZB

BOOKS 2 READ

Connecting independent readers to independent writers.

Did you love *Forehead Kiss*? Then you should read *Holliday Drama*[1] by Jessica Terry!

Triplets Emberly, Evelyn, Enya, and their brother Noah might be up to their eyeballs in holiday traditions and the importance of family, but their respective love lives aren't always so cheerful.

Emberly, the yearning pastry chef, considers her status as 'outcast' among her siblings as justification for the secret she's keeping.

---

1. https://books2read.com/u/38wepw

2. https://books2read.com/u/38wepw

Evelyn can't seem to accept the fact that she's divorced from her high school sweetheart, Travis, and continues to do things that are, well, foolish.

Enya has never had a problem getting a man; she's just never been pressed about keeping one. But when she finds the one she's sure is for her, he doesn't exactly come issue-free.

Serial monogamist Noah has been secretly pining for someone, and he's tired of waiting. One of his sisters might have a major problem with it, though.

All of this will come to a head at some point and when it does, will their 'family over everything' mentality withstand the damage?

Read more at https://www.jessicaterry.com/.

About the Author

Jessica Terry caught the writing bug at a young age and loves little more than holing up at home in Douglasville, GA, cranking out contemporary novels. And eating. www.jessicaterry.com

Read more at https://www.jessicaterry.com/.